The Sleepover Club

Three fantastic Sleepover Club
stories in One!

Have you been invited to all these sleepovers?

1. The Sleepover Club at Frankie's
2. The Sleepover Club at Lyndsey's
3. The Sleepover Club at Felicity's
4. The Sleepover Club at Rosie's
5. The Sleepover Club at Laura's
6. Starring the Sleepover Club
7. Sleepover Girls go Pop!
8. The 24-Hour Sleepover Club
9. The Sleepover Club Sleeps Out
10. Happy Birthday Sleepover Club
11. Sleepover Girls on Horseback
12. Sleepover in Spain
13. Sleepover on Friday 13th
14. Sleepover Girls go Camping
15. Sleepover Girls go Detective
16. Sleepover Girls go Designer
17. The Sleepover Club Surfs the Net
18. Sleepover Girls on Screen
19. Sleepover Girls and Friends
20. Sleepover Girls on the Catwalk
21. The Sleepover Club Goes for Goal!
22. Sleepover Girls go Babysitting
23. Sleepover Girls go Snowboarding
24. Happy New Year, Sleepover Club!
25. Sleepover Girls go Green
26. We Love You Sleepover Club
27. Vive le Sleepover Club!
28. Sleepover Club Eggstravaganza
29. Emergency Sleepover
30. Sleepover Girls on the Range
31. The Sleepover Club Bridesmaids
32. Sleepover Girls See Stars
33. Sleepover Club Blitz
34. Sleepover Girls in the Ring
35. Sari Sleepover
36. Merry Christmas Sleepover Club!
37. The Sleepover Club Down Under
38. Sleepover Girls go Splash!
39. Sleepover Girls go Karting
40. Sleepover Girls go Wild!
41. The Sleepover Club at the Carnival
42. The Sleepover Club on the Beach
43. Sleepover Club Vampires
44. sleepoverclub.com
45. Sleepover Girls go Dancing
46. The Sleepover Club on the Farm
47. Sleepover Girls go Gymtastic!
48. Sleepover Girls on the Ball
49. Sleepover Club Witches
50. Sleepover Club Ponies
51. Sleepover Girls on Safari
52. Sleepover Club Makeover
53. Sleepover Girls go Surfing
54. Sleepover Girls go Treasure Hunting

Mega
Sleepover Club 8

Sleepover Girls See Stars
Sleepover Club Vampires
Sleepover Club Witches

Sue Mongredien
Fiona Cummings
Jana Hunter

Collins

An imprint of HarperCollinsPublishers

The Sleepover Club ® is a
registered trademark of HarperCollins*Publishers* Ltd

Sleepover Girls See Stars first published in Great Britain by Collins 2000
Sleepover Club Vampires first published in Great Britain by Collins 2001
Sleepover Club Witches first published in Great Britain by Collins 2001

First published in this three-in-one edition by Collins 2003

Collins is an imprint of HarperCollins*Publishers* Ltd
77-85 Fulham Palace Road, Hammersmith
London W6 8JB

The HarperCollins website address is
www.harpercollins.co.uk

3 5 7 9 10 8 6 4 2

Sleepover Girls See Stars Text copyright © Sue Mongredien 2000
Sleepover Club Vampires Text copyright © Fiona Cummings 2001
Sleepover Club Witches Text copyright © Jana Hunter 2001

Original series characters, plotlines
and settings © Rose Impey 1997

ISBN 0 00 716491–2

The authors assert the moral right to
be identified as the authors of the work.

Printed and bound in England by
Clays Ltd, St Ives plc

Sleepover Kit List

1. Sleeping bag
2. Pillow
3. Pyjamas or a nightdress
4. Slippers
5. Toothbrush, toothpaste, soap etc
6. Towel
7. Teddy
8. A creepy story
9. Food for a midnight feast:
   chocolate, crisps, sweets, biscuits.
   In fact anything you like to eat.
10. Torch
11. Hairbrush
12. Hair things like a bobble or hairband,
    if you need them
13. Clean knickers and socks
14. Change of clothes for the next day
15. Sleepover diary and membership card

Sleepover Girls
See Stars

An imprint of HarperCollins*Publishers*

CHAPTER ONE

Greetings, earthlings! It's Rosie here – or should I say Carromi?! That's my alien name, before you think I've gone mad! Do you know how to work out your own alien name? It's dead easy.

1) Take the first three letters of your surname (mine's 'c-a-r' from Cartwright).

2) Then take the first two letters of your first name ('r-o', that's easy).

3) And finally, take the first two letters of your mum's maiden name ('m-i' for Millington in my mum's case).

4) Add them all together and there's your new name! Cool, eh?

You're probably wondering two things. Firstly, why am I wibbling on about alien names at all? And secondly, you might be thinking – hang on, *Rosie* doesn't often tell the Sleepover stories! Why's she doing this one?

Well, this is why. The story I'm about to tell is so weird and spooky and freaky that Frankie said no-one would believe her if *she* told it. Everyone would just think, "Yeah, yeah, Frankie and her vivid imagination!" But if I, Rosie the hard-boiled cynic, tell you what happened to us, you might just believe it. So here I am!

So why am I going on about alien names? Well, we've all been getting *reeeeeally* into aliens and UFOs and space and spooky things, lately, ever since Frankie first got the telescope, and...

WHOOPS! You can tell I'm not used to doing this, can't you? I haven't even told you who Frankie is, or even mentioned any of the others yet! Sorry – shall I start again?

I'm Rosie Maria Cartwright and I'm in the Sleepover Club. Do you know the others? I'll never forget the day I met them. My family had just moved to Cuddington and I had to start at Cuddington Primary School without knowing a single person. Have you ever had to start a new school where everyone knows everyone else already, and they all have their own special groups of friends? It was *soooo* horrible. I felt dead lonely and missed all my old mates like mad – until Lyndz took me under her wing, that is.

That's Lyndz for you – she's the kindest person I've ever met. Her alien name is Collyle and she'd come from Planet Nice, if she really was an alien! She'd do anything for anyone, I reckon. Well, she came right up to me in the playground and asked me if I wanted to join in with a skipping game. Then later on she told me all about this Sleepover Club she was in and asked me to join that, too. So I did!

I think the other Sleepover Clubbers were a teensy weensy bit narked about that, actually. They've all known each other since they were babies, practically, and I could tell Frankie and Kenny were sussing me out at first – trying to decide if I was good enough for their club! They must have thought so, luckily, 'cos I've been best mates with all of them ever since. Now I'm just *soooo* glad we moved to Cuddington, as I've got the most excellent friends a girl could ever wish for!

There's three others in our club, apart from Lyndz and me. For starters, there's Frankie Thomas, the crazy one who comes out with these off-the-wall ideas all the time. Planet Bonkers, that's where Frankie – or Thofral – would be from. Honestly, I don't know how she thinks of all her mad plans. She's tall and skinny, very funny and quite bossy. And boy, is she LOUD!

Kenny McKenzie's the sport freak, and if she were an alien, she'd definitely be from Planet Football! Kenny (Mcklali – her real name's Laura) is a bit wild, too. She'd do anything for a dare. Last week, she jumped off Frankie's back wall, which is about ten feet high, just because Frankie bet her 50p she couldn't do it. You can't say things like that to Kenny without her trying to prove you wrong! I couldn't watch as she did it 'cos I was convinced she'd crack her head open or break her leg or something but – whoosh! Down she jumped, cool as anything. Dusted off her shorts – and then went straight into loads of handsprings and cartwheels around the garden. "Show off," Frankie muttered in disgust, as she reached for her purse. "Makes me feel sick just looking at her!"

And last but not least there's Felicity Proudlove, who's from Planet Girly, I reckon. Her alien name should be Prfegr by rights, but as that's far too unpronounceable, we cheated a bit! Fliss's name *used* to be Sidebotham – which, as you can imagine, she hated 'cos all the boys at school called her nicknames. Then her mum remarried last month so Fliss got a new surname – Proudlove, which is almost as bad!

Anyway, just to avoid a total tongue-twister, we decided to bend the rules and use her old surname for her alien name. So now it's Sidfegr, or Sid for short! Don't ask me why, but Fliss is just totally into clothes and make-up and boys and all sorts of boring things like that. She's the only one of the Sleepover Club who'd ever *dream* of kissing pictures of boy bands in magazines, put it like that! I thought

13

Fliss was a bit prim and proper when I first met her, but now I've sussed she's excellent value for teasing big-time. She's like one of those clockwork toys – wind her up and watch her go! She falls for a trick every time. Me and Kenny tease her a lot – it's one of my favourite sports!

Anyway, like I said, we're the Sleepover Club, and as well as seeing each other every day at school, we also have sleepovers every Friday or Saturday at someone's house. Sometimes they're for a specific reason, like if we're planning something special together for a school project or for Brownies. But most of the time, we just play stupid games, muck about, dress up, eat loads of sweets and stay up all night whispering ghost stories. It's *sooo* much fun! Weekends are just the best. No school – and it's Sleepover time!!

Right, I think I've told you all the important bits now. On with the story!

It all started in the school holidays. August! I love that month! It was a really hot, hot, *hot* week, so Frankie suggested an outdoor sleepover at hers for that Friday.

"We can all sleep out in the garden!" she said excitedly. "We can either put up a couple of tents or just sleep in our sleeping bags under the stars!"

"Cool!" we all said, eyes lighting up at the thought. Well – nearly all of us...

"What about insects?" Fliss said at once, looking anxious.

"Well, what about them?" Kenny asked, even though we all knew what was coming.

"They'll crawl on us!" Fliss said, as if we were completely stupid. "They'll crawl on us when we're asleep – they might even crawl into our *mouths*!"

If there's one thing Fliss hates more than the sight of blood, it's creepy-crawlies. They totally freak her out!

"I've never seen that many insects in Frankie's garden," Lyndz said encouragingly. "Anyway, don't *they* sleep at night, too?"

"Oh, no – they love night time," Kenny teased. "They go berserk at night time, crawling and squirming everywhere. And they just *love* crawling into people's mouths – it's their favourite thing. If there's a mouth anywhere around, they'll all be flocking towards it, fast as you like. Queuing up for it, I'm telling you! Straight up!"

"Straight *in*, you mean!" I said. "Yum, yum, delicious!"

Fliss looked as if she was about to cry. "I know you're just trying to scare me," she said. "But now I really *really* don't want to sleep outside!"

"You're not frightened of a few teeny tiny little insects are you, Fliss?" Kenny said. "They can't hurt you!"

"Some of them can," she said defensively. "Some of them bite you. Some of them sting!" Then a look of panic spread over her face. "And what if there are snakes about? A poisonous snake can *kill* you!"

"Oh, snakes are lovely!" Lyndz – or Pet Rescue, as we sometimes call her – said. "But don't worry, there aren't any poisonous ones in this country. Apart from adders, of course."

"One might slither over you," I pointed out cheerfully.

"Or a moth might land on your face like this," Kenny said, tickling Fliss's cheek with a piece of grass.

Fliss batted it away, looking pea-green. "No, I mean it, I can't do it," she said. "I can't sleep outside – it's just too dangerous."

We all burst out laughing.

"Oh, we'll put up a tent for you, then, Indiana Jones," Frankie said. "And if you're still scared, you can sleep in the shed!"

The rest of us were all dead excited about sleeping outside. I crossed my fingers for the whole week, hoping it wouldn't rain. Frankie's garden is huge, much better than ours.

I hate our garden. When my dad moved out, he left our house and garden in a right state. I mean, it was such a *dump*, I was too embarrassed to ask anyone round for ages and ages. He keeps promising to come round and finish doing it up for us and Mum, but now he's got this new girlfriend, he always has a convenient excuse lined up to get out of it. Me and Tiffany, my big sister, have tried doing stuff in the garden to make it a bit nicer – like mowing the lawn and planting some flowers here and there – but it still looks scruffy and boring.

Not like Frankie's. Her mum and dad are quite well-off and her mum loves gardening. Now Frankie's got a baby sister, Izzy, her mum has her hands full but the garden still looks great – in fact, the whole house still looks dead tidy. Still, I suppose it would if you can afford a gardener and a cleaner one day a week...

Anyway, it finally came round to Friday, and I biked over to Frankie's that afternoon. The others were already there, and I could tell when Frankie opened the front door that she was excited about something or other.

"Brilliant! Excellent! You're here," she said breathlessly. "Now I can tell everyone my big surprise!"

"Oh, no," Fliss groaned. "I don't know if I want to hear this!"

"You do," Frankie said. "You all do. I'm proud to announce that tonight, we're having a star-spotting sleepover!"

I blinked. Star-spotting?

"Really?" Fliss said excitedly. "Which stars? Oh, I wish you'd said before! I could have brought my autograph book!"

The look on Frankie's face was so disbelieving, I couldn't help a gurgle of laughter. Then Lyndz started giggling... and that was it! We all were just *roaring* with laughter – except Fliss of course.

"What?" she asked. "What's so funny?!"

"Stars in the SKY, Fliss – not famous people!" Frankie spluttered.

"Oh," said Fliss, going red.

"Yeah, 'cos there are *sooooo* many celebrities wandering around Cuddington, aren't there?" Kenny said sarcastically. "I saw Steps practising dance routines in the park yesterday, and Konnie from *Blue Peter* in the newsagent..."

"All right, all right!" Fliss said, huffily. "It was an easy mistake to make!"

"Anyway, look at this!" Frankie said, changing the subject. "Ta-da!"

She held up a large, heavy-looking black case and then opened it up. "It's a telescope!" she said, her eyes gleaming with excitement. "Mad Uncle Colin gave it me for a birthday present."

"Er… your birthday's in April," I pointed out.

"Yeah, a *late* birthday present," Frankie said. "He picked it up in an antique shop and thought I'd like it." She was fiddling around, putting it together. "Honestly, you can see the stars dead clearly. It's *wicked*!"

Fliss was wrinkling her nose. "And that's what you want us to do tonight – look at stars?" she said. "Doesn't sound much fun to me."

"Yeah, if only the telescope stretched all the way to Hollywood, eh, Fliss," Kenny said cuttingly. "Might be able to see a few *real* stars there!"

Fliss was about to pout but changed her mind and threw a cushion at Kenny instead.

"OK, funny bunny," she said. "Ha ha ha, let's all laugh at Fliss, shall we?"

"Yeah, let's," agreed Kenny. "There's always something to laugh at!"

"OK, you two, cut it out," Lyndz said.

"Yeah, 'cos I haven't even got to the best bit yet," Frankie said dramatically. "Because I've been thinking. With this telescope, we won't just be able to see loads of stars tonight – we might even be able to see UFOs!"

"UF-what?" Fliss asked.

"UFOs – you know, unidentified flying objects!" Frankie said.

Fliss was still looking blank.

Frankie sighed and rolled her eyes. "Aliens, Fliss!" she said. "Aliens!"

CHAPTER TWO

It was me who got the giggles first again. I couldn't help it! Frankie just cracks me up with her stoopid ideas. "Aliens?" I said. "Yeah, right! Little green men, eh, Frank?"

Frankie shrugged. "Why not?" she said. "Don't you watch *The X-Files*?"

"Yeah!" I said. "And that's a TV programme. It's not real, you know!"

"My gran saw a ghost once," Lyndz put in helpfully.

"Ghosts are ghosts," Kenny said. "Frankie's talking about extra-terrestrials. Aliens from another world who can suck out your brain with a single *slurp*..."

"Stop it, Kenny," Fliss ordered. "I know you're trying to spook me again. Well, it won't work!"

"There is a lot of evidence that aliens exist…" Frankie started bossily.

I wasn't having any of that! "A lot of hoaxes, you mean!" I said. "Nothing has ever been proved, Frankie – except that some people have a very vivid imagination!"

Frankie was just about to reply when her mum shouted to us all: "Girls! Tea's ready!"

"Saved by the parent," Frankie muttered, as we went into the kitchen.

But if I thought that was going to be the end of the alien theme, I was wrong! Frankie had been busy all morning making – no, not fairy cakes – *alien* cakes, which were bright green with funny face decorations. Then her mum had continued the idea for the rest of the meal. The egg sandwiches had an extra ingredient of food colouring to make them green, pink and blue, and there was a red jelly that Frankie had mashed up into red, wobbling lumps. "Alien-brain jelly," she proudly informed us.

I saw Fliss look anxiously around the table

for anything vaguely normal, but everything had had the extra-terrestrial treatment. I'll say one thing for Frankie – she doesn't do things by halves! We even had lime cordial – I mean "alien blood" – to drink.

"Right, let's set up the telescope," Frankie said as soon as we finished.

"But it's still light," Kenny pointed out. It wasn't even seven o'clock, right in the middle of summer!

"Do we have to?" moaned Fliss. "Can't we play a game?"

Even Frankie's mum agreed. "You won't be able to see anything yet," she said, clearing the plates away.

Frankie hates having to wait for anything. "OK – why don't we watch a spooky film, to get us in the mood, then?" she said.

"What, *ET*?" I scoffed. "Yeah, that's really scary!"

Kenny looked longingly outside. She hates being cooped up indoors. She's only happy when she's racing about, using up tons of energy, I think. "Why don't we set up camp in the garden?" she said.

Frankie was starting to get a bit rattled. "Not *ET*! And we can sort the camp out later, Kenz," she said. "No, I was thinking of *The X-Files* – you know, the one that was on really late in the week? Mum taped it for me. What do you reckon?"

"As long as *everyone* wants to," Mrs Thomas interrupted. "I don't want anyone to get nightmares tonight."

"Oh, Mum!" Frankie begged. "Go on, please – none of us *ever* gets nightmares, I swear!"

Fliss bit her lip at that point. She gets terrible nightmares sometimes if we've all been telling ghost stories.

Just at that moment, baby Izzy burst into howls.

"Well..." Frankie's mum said, still not totally convinced, but too concerned about Izzy to argue any more. "OK, then."

"Yay!" shouted Frankie, jumping up and down.

"As long as you promise me that if anyone gets too scared, you'll stop the tape, OK?" she said, hurrying out of the room with Izzy.

Frankie winked at us. "Izzy is *soooo* cool!

She's got the knack of crying just when Mum's about to stop me doing something!" she said happily. "Come on – let's watch some *X-Files* action on the box!"

It was a brilliant programme – even if we were hiding behind cushions for a lot of it! I don't think Fliss saw more than ten minutes of it, as she refused point-blank to watch any of the scary bits.

Then, by the time it had finished, it was finally getting dark. Frankie was *soooo* excited. You'd think she'd never seen darkness before!

We went out into the garden to set up camp. It was such a hot evening that me, Kenny, Frankie and Lyndz all wanted to sleep under the stars in our sleeping bags. Fliss was still determined not to, so Frankie threw an old sheet over the washing line and pegged the corners into the ground.

"Da-da! Easiest tent in the world or what?!" she said.

Fliss's face fell. "But snakes can still crawl in through the ends," she pointed out, looking very doubtful about the "easiest tent in the world".

Frankie thought quickly. "But if there are any snakes around, they'll go straight to the pond over there," she said. "Snakes love swimming at night, don't they, Lyndz?"

I could tell Frankie was fibbing and knew nothing whatsoever about snakes' night habits – but Fliss seemed to want to believe it.

"Er, yeah, I think so," Lyndz said, sounding doubtful.

"There you go then!" Frankie said. "They won't bother coming near you when the pond's right over there! Problem solved!"

We all helped set up the telescope. There seemed to be lots of fiddly bits to it, what with all the lenses and the stand and everything.

"Hey, why don't we spy into your neighbours' houses?" Kenny suggested, once it was all set up. "That would be so cool! We could see everything they were up to!"

"Not half as cool as seeing an alien," Frankie said, her eye glued to the end of the telescope. "Right – I've got it lined up to see the Plough – anyone want to have a look?"

"The Plough?" Lyndz asked.

"It's a constellation," Frankie said

importantly. "It's meant to look like the shape of a plough, but if you ask me, it's more like a saucepan."

I had a look, then Lyndz, then Kenny. I couldn't really see the plough-shape myself, but it was quite cool seeing the stars so much clearer.

"Fliss, do you want a look?" Frankie asked.

There was a moment's silence – and we all turned round to look at Fliss, who was reading something in a book with her torch. She looked up. "What did you say?" she asked.

"What's that – *My Big Book of Insects*?" Kenny said, trying to read the cover. "*The Alien-Spotter's Guide to Mars*?"

Fliss held it up so we could see. *Virgo – Your Daily Stars in 2000*, it was called. "It's my horoscopes book," she said solemnly. "I got it half-price in a sale. Good eh?"

"Half-price?" I snorted. "I'm not surprised – over half the year's gone already!"

"Yeah, but I've read my horoscopes for all the days that have already gone as well," she said defensively.

"Well, what's the point of that?" Kenny

asked. She's as cynical as me when it comes to airy-fairy things like horoscopes. What a load of old rubbish!

Fliss gave this knowing sort of smile. "Well, the point is, Kenny, that everything in here has come true!" she said. "Take last month – Rosie's birthday."

"What, your horoscopes book knew it was my birthday?" I said sarcastically. "Let's have a look!"

I grabbed it off her and read the entry for my birthday, July 15th. "'A good day for being with friends and family'," I read aloud. "'There may be something to celebrate.'" I passed the book back to her. "Big deal!" I said. "You see your family every day anyway – and you see us most days, too. So what?"

"'Something to celebrate' – that was your birthday," Fliss persisted. "And I spent the day with friends – we all went to the park, didn't we? See! It's all true!"

I caught Kenny's eye, and we both shook our heads, grinning. Fliss is just *soooo* gullible! She's a sucker for anything like that.

"So what are your stars for today?" Lyndz

asked quickly before either of us could make any more horrible remarks.

"Well, that's what I was just reading," Fliss said. "It's quite an exciting one today. 'Watch out for something unexpected. A new cycle begins today, and seeing is definitely believing'." She closed the book with a snap. "Sounds good, eh?"

"'A new cycle' – does that mean your step-dad's fixed your bike?" Kenny said.

"'Something unexpected' – that probably means a moth flying into your mouth," I teased. "Doesn't sound much fun to me!"

I could tell Frankie was getting bored of this conversation. "That's enough about your stars, Fliss," she said. "Let's get back to the REAL stars again! Do you want a look?"

"Watch out for something unexpected, remember!" Kenny teased as Fliss put her book down. "Something totally unexpected – like the moon!"

"Shut up, Kenny!" Fliss said, sticking her nose in the air.

"Oh, ignore her," Lyndz said. "She's just jealous of your exciting horoscope, Fliss!"

30

"Mmm, yeah, absolutely," Kenny said, sticking her tongue out. "Ooh, I'm *soooo* jealous!"

Fliss put one eye to the telescope and shut the other. Her hands came around the telescope to hold it steady. "Wow!" she said. "Stars!"

Then she looked over at Kenny triumphantly. "See? That was unexpected. I had no idea I was going to be looking through a telescope today – the book was right!"

Kenny threw a jelly baby at Fliss, which bounced straight off her head. "And *that* was something *else* unexpected!" she said. "Now all you need is to get your bike fixed and the whole horoscope will be right!"

"Oh shut up!" Fliss said crossly, and swung the telescope round so it was pointing at Kenny. Then she giggled. "Eurgh, Kenny, I can see right up your nose!" she said. "And I think you've got a spot coming on your forehead!"

"Don't swing it around like that, Fliss!" Frankie said sternly. "It's meant to point up at the sky! Why do you want to look even closer at Kenny's ugly mug, anyway?"

"Sorry, Frankie," Fliss said, and started moving the telescope back up towards the stars again. Then she stopped and peered through the lens, frowning at something. "What on earth is THAT?" she muttered to herself. "There aren't any *green* stars, are there?"

We all looked at each other. What was Fliss on about now?

"Ooh, it's moving up and down now," she said excitedly. "Frankie – quick, come and look at this!"

Frankie was over in a shot, and grabbed the telescope off her.

"I don't believe it!" she murmured, peering through. "I just don't believe it! There really is something there! Green flashing lights – moving up and down!" She stood back and looked at us, her mouth hanging open. "Quick, all of you, look!"

We each looked at the green lights in turn. I was the last one to look and, to be honest, I didn't think for a minute it would be anything weird. But sure enough, I did see the green lights Fliss had spotted moving slowly up in the air, and then down again. Then they vanished.

"They've gone!" I said, moving the telescope up and down, trying to spot them again. "They seemed to go down – and then just disappeared."

Frankie was practically jumping up and down in excitement. "I can't believe we've seen a spaceship!" she squeaked. "I just can't believe we saw it!"

"Now, wait a minute..." I said. No-one had said anything about a spaceship until then.

"Aliens!" Frankie said. "Here in Cuddington!" She stood and looked in the direction the telescope was pointing. "That's Cuddington Hill over there," she said. "What if aliens have landed on Cuddington Hill?!"

CHAPTER THREE

We all stared at each other in disbelief.

"*I* saw them first," Fliss said importantly – and then her eyes went wide. "See? THAT must have been what my horoscope book was talking about. Aliens! I mean, how unexpected can you get?!"

"That is completely and totally and utterly unexpected," Lyndz agreed solemnly.

There was a moment's silence while we all thought about it.

"So if aliens have landed in Cuddington," Kenny said slowly and dramatically, "how long have we got before they get off their ship and come to get us?"

We all looked at each other and screamed at the same time – even me!

"There's no way on earth I'm sleeping out here now!" Fliss said, grabbing her book and sleeping bag. "No way!"

"Nor me," said Lyndz, shuddering. "I don't want to be an alien breakfast!"

"Quick!" Frankie said. "Abandon mission – now!"

We grabbed our sleeping bags and pillows, and Frankie picked up the telescope and we ran into the house as fast as possible. Safely inside the kitchen, we all jumped around screeching hysterically. Whether it was aliens or not, SOMETHING had definitely landed on Cuddington Hill – and none of us fancied sleeping outside to find out WHAT!

Now you can say what you like about me, but one thing I'm not is superstitious. I don't really believe in any of that black cat, walking under ladders, two magpies stuff for starters – and I certainly don't believe in fairies, witches, ghosts and aliens! Yet suddenly I was feeling just as spooked as all the others. I really

REALLY didn't want to sleep in the garden, that was for sure, even though I was convinced there had to be a perfectly good explanation for seeing those green lights on Cuddington Hill. I mean, this was the twenty-first century after all!

But you know when everyone around you is getting really scared, and you've just seen a creepy TV programme, and there's a little voice in your head saying "What if...?" Well, that's what I was feeling – that delicious kind of scared, jumpy feeling in my tummy. I mean, what if we really *had* seen something weird? What then? Even though I knew deep down that aliens were just something you saw in films, the creepy feeling, plus the hysteria of all the others, was really getting to me!

Of course, Frankie's mum and dad weren't having any of it.

"I knew this would happen if you watched that programme!" Mrs Thomas said, sounding annoyed. "You watch a programme about aliens – and then you're convinced you've seen aliens in Cuddington! What a coincidence!"

Put like that, of course, it did sound a bit daft.

"I know what I saw, Mum," Frankie said defiantly. "And we ALL saw it, so there!"

Frankie's dad thought the whole thing was hilarious. "Ooh, look, girls – the TV reception has gone a bit fuzzy," he said. "Must be the alien landing interfering with transmission!"

"Da-a-a-a-ad!" Frankie said crossly. "Don't blame us if the body-snatchers come in the night, then!"

"I promise I won't blame you," he said, trying not to smile. "Now I think you five should transport yourselves to bed. And Frankie..."

"Yes, Dad?"

"Make sure your bedroom window's closed." He winked at us. "We wouldn't want anything clambering in there while you're asleep, would we?"

I laughed at that, but I thought Fliss was going to faint, she looked so white.

"Why did he have to say that?" she whispered as we were going upstairs. "I'll NEVER be able to sleep now!"

"At least there aren't any snakes or insects in Frankie's bedroom," Lyndz pointed out comfortingly.

"I think I'd rather have a few insects than green slimy aliens!" Fliss said with a shudder. "Bagsy me not sleeping by the window!"

"Turn around, touch the ground, bagsy not me!" Lyndz said quickly.

In the end we had to toss for it, because no-one really wanted to sleep by the window, not even fearless Frankie and Kenny! Frankie lost the toss – but she persuaded her mum to let Pepsi the dog sleep in there with us, just to protect us from anything scary.

It was just about impossible to get to sleep that night. Normally on sleepover nights, as you can imagine, we don't fall asleep until really really late anyway because we're always whispering silly things to each other or telling jokes, or sometimes Kenny tells one of her grisly ghost stories to scare us.

But on this particular night, every time there was the teeniest tiniest noise, Fliss sat bolt upright in the darkness and said, "What was THAT?"

"Mum and Dad in the kitchen," Frankie would say, or "A car outside," or "The wind in the trees."

Suddenly there came this low humming sound, so low you had to really strain your ears to hear it. Then it stopped.

"W-w-w-what was that?" Kenny asked. Even *she* sounded scared now.

No-one could think of anything it might have been.

"It's probably nothing," I said. I was trying to sound brave but my voice had a definite wobble to it.

Then the humming started again. Very very faint. We all lay as still as still, listening to it. There's something about the darkness that makes noises sound even scarier than usual, do you know what I mean?

"What do you think it is?" Fliss whispered.

Again it stopped.

"I think it's the spaceship hovering outside," Kenny whispered, and Fliss let out a muffled scream as she pulled her sleeping bag right over her head.

Then there was a giggle. A Kenny giggle.

"Mmmmm," she hummed loudly and giggled some more. "Got you all there, didn't I?" she laughed. "Mmmmm – quick, the spaceship's getting nearer!"

I rolled over on top of her. "You evil cow!" I said, starting to giggle myself – in sheer relief as much as anything! "Come on, you lot – pile on!"

"You mean it was you all along?!" Fliss said indignantly, poking her head out of the sleeping bag again. "Right! You're gonna pay for that, McKenzie!"

We all piled on to Kenny until she begged for mercy. "No – aaargh! Stop! Mercy! Mercy!" she squeaked breathlessly. "I'm sorry – I couldn't resist!"

We all got a bad case of the giggles after that. It was that nervous sort of giggling where you just can't stop yourself.

Then there was a tap at the door.

"Aaaargh!" we all screamed, and burst out giggling again.

"Girls, it's half past eleven," called Mr Thomas through the door. "Any more racket and I'll send the aliens in to keep you quiet!"

That just made us even worse! Trying to giggle quietly is just *soooo* difficult! I had to put some of my sleeping bag in my mouth to try and keep the volume down, but I had Lyndz clutching me, shaking with laughter on one side, and I could feel Frankie heaving with giggles on the other.

"I need some sweets to calm me down," Lyndz said weakly after a few minutes.

"Yeah, chocolate, good idea!" Kenny said. "Stuff some in your mouth and you won't be able to laugh so much!"

We all had a bit of Frankie's huge Dairy Milk bar that she'd bought, and sure enough, as the chocolate melted in our mouths, I started to feel a bit better.

"I wonder what it was we saw tonight," I said, feeling a bit sleepier. "Maybe it was just a low-flying plane."

"A low-flying plane that goes up and down with green lights on it?" Frankie snorted. "Do me a favour!"

"What do you think aliens look like?" Fliss wondered aloud.

"Probably a bit like you," Kenny said

cheekily. "A bit better-looking though, I should think…"

Whoomp! Fliss chucked her teddy bear over at Kenny. I forgot to tell you, Fliss is actually *reeeeaaaallly* pretty – but doesn't she just know it! Long blonde hair and big blue eyes, you know the sort. She's got the type of face that grannies always make comments about when they see her. "Ooh, isn't she an angel?", that sort of thing.

"Teddy fight!" said Kenny in a low voice, chucking hers at Lyndz. Soon there were teddies flying in all directions through the darkness. Pepsi got a bit excited and started barking and running around, trying to catch one in his mouth.

"Pepsi, get off!" Lyndz giggled. "Ugh, he's slobbered all over Barnaby!"

"Keep it down in there, girls!" shouted Mr Thomas again. "Last warning, Frankie!"

Once we'd all calmed down, Frankie was the first one to speak. "I know it's late now and we should get to sleep," she whispered. "But all I want to say is this. I don't know what we saw out there tonight, but I have this strange feeling that it was something really freaky that we just happened to stumble upon. Anyway, whatever it was, I know one thing for sure. Tomorrow morning we're going to go to Cuddington Hill and have a good look around. Because I for one want to get to the bottom of this!"

"Me too," said Kenny.

"Me three," said Lyndz.

"Me four," said Fliss. "But only if it's not going to be too scary," she added quickly.

There was a silence while I thought about it. Why not? I *was* starting to feel pretty curious about the whole thing myself.

"Me five," I said. "So we're all in it together!"

CHAPTER FOUR

Even though, like I told you, I don't believe in alien stuff, I found that I couldn't get to sleep that night. The little "What if...?" voice just wouldn't go away. What if we'd really stumbled upon something? We could be famous all over the world if we'd really spotted an alien spaceship. We might even get to be on telly and everything!

Then the sensible voice would start. Of course it wasn't an alien spaceship. There was no such thing! So there had to be a logical explanation. But what?

In the end, my poor brain got so exhausted from all its weird thoughts, I finally managed to get some shut-eye. But even then, my dreams were full of flashing lights and little green men – all those things I'd been so scornful about earlier! It really was a strange kind of night.

Next morning, it was still the only thing we could talk about.

"I couldn't stop dreaming about aliens last night," Lyndz said in a low voice, pouring Cheerios into a bowl at the breakfast table. "And in one dream, there was this green slimy figure that kept talking to me. Telling me to do things – and then I couldn't help doing everything it said! Spooky, eh?"

"Did it tell you to pass the milk over to me?" Kenny said, grinning. "Oh, no, I just told you that, didn't I?"

Fliss was spreading jam on her toast, and not saying much. She looked really tired – I guessed she hadn't slept very well either.

"In my dream, an alien shot straight out of your stomach, Kenz," Frankie said lightly, taking a big bite of toast. "Just like in *The X-Files*. It was gr-r-r-ross!"

Kenny looked down at her tummy. "I

thought I felt something squirming about in there," she said cheerfully, and gave it a pat. "I thought it was just my Rice Krispies snapping, crackling and popping away!"

Fliss pulled a sick face. "Kenny, do you have to?" she said. "I don't want to think about an alien coming out of you – not when you're sitting right next to me, anyway!"

"I wonder if THAT's in your horoscope book?" Kenny teased. "'Today you will be shocked by an alien's head emerging from your friend's stomach...' Now if your book said that, it WOULD impress me!"

"So is everyone still up for going over to Cuddington Hill today?" I asked as Fliss picked up her horoscope book to check her stars. "Not that I believe for a minute that there's any alien goings-on, of course – but it would be good just to check that there's nothing freaky up there."

"And it would be even better to see that there IS something freaky up there!" Frankie said happily. "Watch out, you extra-terrestrials – the Sleepover Club is coming to check you out!"

"I wonder if the aliens are friendly?" Lyndz pondered.

"Oh, I doubt it," Kenny said. "Probably the head-tearing-off type. Did you see that film where—"

"Uh-oh," Fliss said loudly. She put her book down, looking worried. "My stars say that I'm to 'tread carefully' today. Do you think that means we shouldn't go up to the hill?"

"Not on your nelly!" Frankie said. "Wild horses couldn't keep me away!"

"What about wild aliens?" I asked with a giggle.

"The wilder the better!" Kenny said. "Come on – eat up, everyone! I want my first ride in a spaceship and I want it now!"

Luckily we all had our bikes with us, which made it a lot easier to get to Cuddington Hill. Frankie and Kenny raced ahead as usual, both wanting to get there first. Me, Lyndz and Fliss went along slower behind them.

Both Frankie and Kenny have got really flash mountain bikes with loads of gears, whereas me and Lyndz have got old hand-me-down cronks that my older sister and her older brothers had before us. So once those two get going, we haven't got a chance of keeping up.

Fliss's bike is pretty nice, too, but she doesn't like going very fast – one, because she hates getting her hair blown about too much, and two, because she says high speeds make her feel sick. But then again, EVERYTHING makes Fliss feel sick, so that's not really surprising!

As soon as Kenny and Frankie were out of sight, Fliss put her brakes on and stopped.

"What's up?" I called over my shoulder. I thought she must have a puncture or something. Me and Lyndz walked our bikes back to her.

"Is your bike OK?" Lyndz asked.

"It's not my bike – it's this whole thing about looking for aliens," Fliss said, looking anxious. "Do you really think it's such a good idea? I can't help thinking about what my horoscopes book warned…"

"Oh, stuff your horoscopes book!" I said. "C'mon, Fliss – one for all and all for one, eh?

Anyway, if you ask me, this whole alien thing is a load of rubbish. There's no such thing! We'll get to Cuddington Hill and you and me can have a good old laugh at Frankie for believing in such nonsense. How about that?"

She still didn't look convinced.

"Come on, Fliss," Lyndz said. "Rosie's right. It's probably nothing. Just think how much better you're going to feel when we find nothing there."

"No more awful scary dreams," I said encouragingly. "Think about it!"

I could see she liked the sound of that idea.

"OK," she said finally, throwing a leg over her bike again. "Let's do it. Let's prove the 'no-alien' theory!"

So off we went again. It was an absolute stonker of a day – bright blue sky and not even a *wisp* of cloud around. It was gorgeous to get a breeze blowing through my hair. Every time we went down a hill, I took my feet off the pedals and stuck them out to the sides. *Wheeeeee!*

We met Frankie and Kenny at the park gates.

"About time!" Frankie said.

I could see Fliss's face turning a bit pink.

"Sorry, Fliss thought she had a puncture but it was OK after all," I said quickly, and she shot me a grateful look. See! I'm not horrible to our Sidfegr ALL the time!!

We pushed our bikes up to the top of Cuddington Hill. It's such a steep hill, not even Kenny fancied her chances cycling up it! "If it was cold, I would," she said, as we puffed our way up the hill. "But as it's so boilingly hot today – no chance!"

"Have you noticed how there's not many people around?" Frankie said. "I wonder if the aliens have been kidnapping a few?"

"Well, it IS nearly lunchtime, I suppose..." Kenny said. "They're probably a bit on the peckish side."

I rolled my eyes. "You two! You're going to be *soooo* disappointed when you realise that actually there were no aliens in Cuddington last night!"

"And YOU are going to be even more disappointed when an alien gobbles you up for being a non-believer!" Frankie retorted.

"Yeah, while me and Frank are worshipped

and crowned queens among the aliens because we believed in them all along!" Kenny said, sticking her tongue out.

I opened my mouth to reply – but just then there was an unmistakable *squelch*!

I turned round to see where it had come from.

Uh-oh...

"Oh, NO!" groaned Fliss. "My new Nikes! Look at them!"

We all just fell about laughing to see that Fliss had trodden straight in a pile of horse poo. It was all over her gleaming white trainers and her face was an absolute picture.

"Trust you, big-foot!" Frankie giggled. "I think your feet have got a poo-magnet on them – you're ALWAYS treading in it!"

"Why do they let horses in this park anyway?" Fliss was fuming. "Nasty great things, pooing everywhere! Ugh! And it STINKS!!"

I had to put my bike down and roll on the grass, I was so helpless with laughter. "Oh, Fliss," I gurgled, "your horoscope DID tell you to 'tread carefully', didn't it?!"

Fliss glared at me as she tried to scrape it off on to the path. "Ugh! Stupid horses!"

"Horses can't help it if they want to poo!" Lyndz said hotly. She's a mad keen rider, so doesn't like ANY criticism of her favourite animal! "You should look where you're going!"

"Good old Fliss," Kenny chortled merrily. "We can always count on you to tread carefully, can't we?"

"Oh, button it, Kenny!" Fliss snapped. "I wish we'd never come on this *stooo*pid bike ride in the first place!"

We carried on up the hill. Fliss was in a total strop, and the rest of us kept bursting into giggles every time we saw her indignant face. Fliss has one of the most expressive faces I've ever seen – and when she's in a bad mood, the whole world knows about it!

We carried on in silence until we got to the top. It was so steep, I could hardly speak with all my huffing and puffing!

Kenny, of course, still had bags of energy. She started running with her bike, then dumped it on the ground once she'd reached the top of the hill. "Come on, you lot!" she yelled, then ran off ahead to look for clues.

We trudged along behind – and then Kenny gave an excited shout. "Quick! Come and look at this!"

CHAPTER FIVE

Suddenly, my legs didn't feel quite so tired any more. We all dropped our bikes in a heap and chased up the rest of the hill to see what she'd found.

"Look! Look! Scorch marks on the grass!" she was yelling. "This must be where the spaceship landed!"

We all knelt on the grass to look closer. Sure enough, there were three or four marks, about thirty centimetres long, where the grass was brown and burned.

"This is proof," Frankie said excitedly. "I've never seen anything like it! This is definite proof!"

She took out her camera and started taking lots of pictures of the scorched grass. "Even *you've* got to admit that this is proof, Rosie!"

I shook my head. "Sorry, Frank. Anything could have scorched that grass," I said. "Doesn't mean it's a spaceship. Anyway – those marks aren't very long, are they? Are you telling me that the spaceship was that small?"

"The scorch marks could be from its feet as it landed," Lyndz pointed out. "Or from some sort of exhaust pipe, you know, like on cars? They always get really hot, don't they?"

She was sounding just as excited as Frankie and Kenny.

"And the aliens might shrink themselves to travel around, anyway," Frankie said. "Travel light, that's what my gran always says!"

I still wasn't convinced one bit!

"There's nothing about those marks that says 'spaceship' to me," I said. I was actually feeling the teensiest bit disappointed, I've got to admit. "What do you reckon, Fliss?"

Fliss's eyes were wide and frightened. "You said there'd be nothing up here, Rosie – and there is!" she said. She sounded quite accusing. She'd obviously really been wanting NOT to have to believe in the spaceship idea. "You can't prove there was nothing there last night now, can you?"

I shrugged impatiently. "This is plain daft!" I said. "A few scorch marks on the grass and you're all freaking out on me! Give me some more proof then – I bet you any money you can't!"

Frankie was scrabbling on the ground. "Oh no?" she said triumphantly. "What's THIS, then?"

We all went over to have a look. In Frankie's hand there was a small, round, flat disc. It looked a bit like a tiddlywink, but it was a bright, shimmering green colour.

"Cool or what?" Frankie said as we all stared at it.

Fliss looked she was going to cry. "I've NEVER seen anything like that before," she said. "Rosie – quick, tell me what it is!"

I grabbed it out of Frankie's hand and peered at it.

"I'm not sure," I said slowly, turning it over

in my hand. "It looks like something out of a board game."

"Oh, yeah, so who's going to come up to the top of Cuddington Hill and play a board game – oh, and at the same time, scorch the grass a few times?" Kenny said ultra-sarcastically. "Hmmm... how about no-one?!"

To be honest, I was totally baffled. I was racking my brain trying to think of a logical explanation but nothing was coming. "Er..." I said, lamely.

"Maybe it's an alien coin," Lyndz said breathlessly. "Maybe one of them dropped it by mistake."

"Wicked! I wonder what we could buy with this?" Frankie said, grabbing it back from me. "A laser gun, maybe, or even a return trip to Mars!"

"I don't like this," Fliss muttered. "I don't like this one bit! I KNEW we shouldn't have come up here. First I tread in horse muck, and then we find an alien coin."

Then a thought struck her, and she looked even more upset. "And what if the aliens want it BACK? What if they come to find us so they can take it back? And it might not be a coin – it might be a... a baby alien, for all we know!"

Fliss was gibbering like a maniac, but Frankie and Kenny just seemed even more excited by the idea.

"I'll look after it!" Kenny said at once, her hand shooting out to snatch the disc.

"No, you will not!" Frankie said immediately, shoving the disc in her pocket. "Finders keepers, losers weepers – so there!"

"Frankie, are you sure you want to look after it?" Lyndz said, sounding nervous. "What if Fliss is right – what if an alien comes to take it back?"

"Then I will be the happiest girl in Cuddington!" Frankie said, grinning. "In fact, I'm really REEEEALLY hoping an alien DOES come to take it back. It would be awesome! Can you imagine?!"

"Can I have another look at it?" I asked. By now, I was desperate to be able to prove it was nothing extra-terrestrial. I just couldn't go along with this alien thing like the others – there *had* to be an explanation to it all.

I peered at the disc again. It was very light in

my hand – I wasn't sure if it was made of metal or what. It had a slight metallic sheen to it, but felt very warm on my skin, not cold like normal metals.

I handed it back, pulling a face. "I'm totally in the dark," I admitted. "I'm sure it's nothing to do with a spaceship, but..."

"So what is it, then, smarty-pants?" crowed Kenny.

I shook my head. "That's the problem," I said. "I just don't know!"

We hunted around for a while longer to see if there were any more clues, but no-one could find anything. I was quite relieved, to be honest. My brain had quite enough to be working on as it was!

When it got to about midday, it was starting to feel really hot on top of the hill.

"Anyone fancy going for a swim this afternoon?" Kenny said, blowing her fringe out of her eyes.

"Yes!" Fliss said at once. "Let's get away from this spooky place – it's giving me the creeps."

"Hold your horses," Frankie said. "I think we should make notes of all our evidence first."

She held up a notebook. "This was going to be a star-spotting notebook, but I think it's going to have to be an alien-spotting book now!"

"Coo-*ell*!" Kenny said. "What are you going to put in it?"

"Well, while we're up here, I'm going to sketch a picture of these scorch marks," she said, turning to the first page.

I pulled a face. "That'll be an interesting picture!" I said sarcastically.

"It's the sort of thing Sherlock Holmes would do," Lyndz said. "You never know, it might jog our memories later on."

"And when I get my film developed, we can stick the pictures in, too," Frankie said. "Now, how long would you say that mark was?"

While the others discussed the marks, I stared into space, thinking how hot it was. And then I saw two girls, about our age, one tall and thin, one small and chubby, coming up the hill towards us, looking very hot and bothered as they made the last steep climb.

"Look! It's the M&Ms!" I said to the others. "What do you think they're doing here?"

In case you didn't know, the M&Ms are Emily Berryman and Emma Hughes – our biggest enemies at school. They are the most absolutely vile, hideous, yucky people in the world, and we always seem to be getting into trouble with them. Luckily, both Ms are a bit dim so we can usually get one over on them, but it has been known for them to trick *us* just as horribly at times!

"Quick, hide the book!" Kenny told Frankie. "We don't want them knowing what we're up to."

"Yeah, no-one say a word about it," Frankie said, stuffing the notebook into her pocket. "Here they come!"

Out of the corner of my eye, I just happened to catch sight of my water bottle on my bike. It's one of those ones with a built-in straw so you can drink while you cycle. Hmm! I thought. Maybe if....

I pulled it off the front of my bike and showed Kenny. "What do you reckon? Super-squirter water pistol or what?"

"I like it!" Kenny said, grabbing hers. "Anyone else got one? Those two look as if they need cooling down a bit!"

From where we were, right on top of the hill, we were in a brilliant spot to get the M&Ms. As soon as they rounded the corner and came into view, Frankie shouted, "Aim... fire!" and all five of us squirted our water bottles at them, *right* into their faces!

I've never seen anyone look more shocked in their lives! Emily and Emma both squealed as they got hit by five streams of water. Within seconds they were totally drenched!

"I might have known it was you lot!" Emily raged. "Look what you've done to my hair! I've just come back from the hairdressers, you know!"

We all burst into giggles at their angry faces and flattened hair.

"I think the 'wet look' looks even better on you!" spluttered Kenny. "Anyway, must dash – things to do, you know..."

We picked up our bikes and raced off down the hill again, away from the furious Ms. They were still so puffed out from climbing the hill that they didn't even have the energy to chase after us.

"Nice work, team," Kenny chuckled as we skidded all the way down. "Did you see their faces? Did we surprise them or WHAT?!"

At the bottom of the hill, we collapsed in a heap of giggles.

"They looked *soooo* mad!" Lyndz spluttered. "They're really going to be out to get us back now!"

"Oh, tremble, tremble!" I said. "Because they're so scary – not!"

"That was fun, wasn't it?" Fliss said happily. "Apart from my trainers getting ruined, of course. Did you finish writing everything up, Frankie?"

"Just about," Frankie said. "What a great day this is turning out to be! Finding clues to an alien landing *and* winding up the M&Ms!"

"Well, we still haven't really proved anything about this so-called alien landing," I said cautiously.

"We've proved that we've got to check THIS out further," Frankie said, still fiddling with the green disc. "And we've proved that, for the first time, the Sleepover Club are stumped! And I HATE being stumped!"

"We definitely need to keep an eye on this hill," Lyndz agreed. "Maybe we'll see the spaceship again – and you never know, next time, we might find something else that even *Rosie* believes in!"

"Next sleepover, we'll definitely have to have another star-spotting session," Frankie said. "It's a date!"

CHAPTER SIX

The next week was the last week of the school holidays. BOOO! Why do the summer holidays whizz by *soooo* quickly? One minute you've got weeks and weeks of no school stretching ahead of you – and the next minute, boom! It's all over and you've got to get your school uniform on again. Gutted!

The last week of the holidays went by quickest of all, of course, and I hardly got a chance to see the others. I went down to the river a couple of times with my brother Adam, who loves fishing.

I don't know if any of the others have told you, but Adam's in a wheelchair 'cos he's got cerebral palsy. That means he can't walk and he can't talk very well either, although he's got this computerised voice box which makes him sound a bit like something out of Star Wars, if you ask me. He can do a wicked Darth Vader impression without even trying!

Some people feel sorry for my brother when they see him and he gets a bit sick of that. I don't feel sorry for him one bit, because most of the time, he's trying to wind me up. He's all right really, though – for a boy!

The rest of the week was dead busy – seeing Dad and Granny and Grandpa, going shopping with my mum for new school shoes... you know what it can be like. It felt like I was in a bit of a whirl with all the family stuff and getting ready for school again. So I was *reeeally* glad when it was finally Friday and we could have another sleepover at Frankie's!

It was actually Kenny's turn to have the sleepover but Frankie got all bossy about her telescope and said she didn't want to have to drag it round to anyone else's house. I reckon that was just an excuse to have the sleepover at hers again!

Kenny didn't mind though – it can be a bit of a nightmare staying at her house 'cos her horrible sister Molly always tries to wreck our sleepovers. So Frankie's it was, then!

This time, there was no waiting till it got dark. By the time the rest of us got round there, around four that afternoon, Frankie had already set up the telescope – or 'Mission Control' as she insisted on calling it! – in the back garden. She had also set up a little camping table and chair by the telescope, complete with paper and different coloured pens.

"Well, like my gran says, if you're going to do something, you may as well do it right!" she said importantly.

Fliss waved her horoscope book in the air. "I have a feeling something may happen again tonight," she said mysteriously. "My horoscope for today says, 'the plot thickens' – I'm sure that means we'll see those lights again!"

"Or even be visited by the aliens, trying to get their coin back," Kenny said, with a wicked grin.

Frankie looked disappointed. "All week I've been hoping they would come for it," she said. "And there's absolutely nothing! Not even one little teeny tiny alien landing on Melford Road! So unfair!"

"Ooh, they're just *sooo* unreliable, aren't they?" I said sarcastically. "So what shall we play while we wait for it to get dark?"

"How about Alien Footsteps?" said Kenny. "It's a bit like Grandmother's Footsteps – but the grandmother is an alien!"

I could see there was going to be NO let-up from aliens that night! Even Fliss seemed to be well into the idea now – especially since her horoscope book was predicting further action!

Once we'd had a few energetic rounds of Alien Footsteps – where Kenny insisted on being the alien that chased the loser (Frankie) round the garden – Fliss pulled a box out of her sleepover bag.

"You're not the only one to get a birthday present this month, Frankie," she said. "Look at this!"

"Your birthday's NEXT month," Lyndz said. "How come you opened it early?"

Fliss looked a bit sheepish. "Well, at home, they've all been calling me Mystic Flisstic, 'cos of my horoscope book," she said, "and—"

"Mystic Flisstic! I like it!" Kenny laughed. "I'm afraid that is your new nickname with us too now, Mystic!"

"Yeah, yeah," said Fliss, tossing her hair. She'd obviously been hearing that nickname a LOT! "Well, anyway, Andy found this in Cuddington Market and said I ought to have it early, so I could use it tonight. 'Cos I've told them all about the aliens, you see, and…"

"So what is it?" Frankie said impatiently. "The suspense is killing us, Flisstic!"

Fliss pulled out a black plastic ball, about the size of a grapefruit, and held it up in the air dramatically. "This is the Magic-8 ball," she said solemnly.

"Ace, can we use it for a football?" Kenny asked.

"Don't you dare!" Fliss cried, clutching it to her chest protectively.

"Didn't Bart have one of those on *The Simpsons*?" I asked. I was sure I'd seen one before.

"Yes! The fortune-telling ball!" Lyndz said. "I've seen that one!"

"Is that what it is, Fliss?" Frankie asked. "Does it tell your fortune?"

"Well, sort of," Fliss said. "You have to ask it a question. Then I turn it upside down and the answer pops up."

"What's the capital of China?" Kenny asked the ball at once. "Who's the manager of Leicester City football club? And what's my middle name?"

"It doesn't answer *that* sort of question!" Lyndz said.

"How convenient!" I muttered under my breath.

"It's yes-no questions only," Fliss said. "Things like, will I marry Ryan Scott?"

She turned the ball upside down and we all peered over her shoulder to look. A message floated up to the surface. "It is decidedly so," the message read.

"Yeeeeessss!" screeched Fliss.

If you didn't know, Ryan Scott is this boy in our class at school that Fliss gets a bit silly over. Yeee-awwwwwn!

"OK, OK, let me ask one," Frankie said. "Was it really an alien spaceship that we saw last week?"

Fliss tipped the ball over, and then back again. Up popped another message. "Yes," was all it said.

"Yo, Mystic Flisstic!" Frankie cheered happily. "I like what you're telling me!"

Me and Kenny exchanged looks, not quite so convinced about the magical powers of this plastic ball.

"OK, I've got one," Kenny said. "Is Fliss going to get eaten by an alien tonight?"

Fliss glared at her. "You can't ask things like that!" she said crossly.

"I just did," Kenny said. "Could the ball answer me, please?"

She winked at me and I grinned back. We were both REEEALLY hoping the ball would say yes again!

Fliss was looking dead miffed – she knew exactly what we were up to. But she tipped the ball upside down obediently.

I crossed my fingers as the answer floated up to the surface.

"Sorry, not today," was the answer.

"Ha ha!" Fliss said triumphantly. "See! The magic ball knows its stuff!"

"Not TODAY, it says," I pointed out. "So it still might happen tonight!"

Fliss shook her head, really chuffed that the so-called magic ball hadn't let her down this time. "I don't think so, girls," she said, smug as anything. "Anyone else got a *proper* question?"

We messed about with the ball for a bit longer, then had tea, then set up Frankie's bedroom for the night. No-one had mentioned wanting to sleep outside tonight – I wonder why?!

"We could even look through the telescope from up in your bedroom, Frankie," scaredy-cat Fliss suggested. "Just in case... in case we see anything scary. Then at least we'll be safe inside!"

"No chance!" Frankie said scornfully. "It'll be much more exciting out in the dark again!"

Fliss looked gloomy. "I knew you'd say that!" she said. "It was worth a try though!"

"Ooh, Mystic Flisstic predicts the future again!" teased Lyndz.

We got our sleeping bags and started laying them out in a line.

"Hey, you know what we haven't done for ages, don't you?" I said suddenly. "Squishy-poo fighting! Anyone fancy a quick game?"

"Top idea!" Kenny said, quickly stuffing her pyjamas and pillow into her sleeping bag to make a big floppy 'squishy-poo'. "Ready or not, here I come!"

Fliss screamed as Kenny whacked her round the head with the squishy-poo.

You've *got* to play this game! It's our very own invention where you stuff your sleeping bag with pillows, teddies, cushions, clothes, anything squashy – and then you go into battle with the others! The winner is the last one to fall over. It is AWESOME fun!

"Aaargh!"

"Help!"

"Gerroffff!"

Bish, bash, bosh! I managed to clobber Frankie from behind, then squishy-poo'd Lyndz right in the mush. Fliss made a surprise comeback and flattened Kenny with hers – so it was just me and Fliss left.

Biff! Pow! Wallop! I jumped on Frankie's bed to give me a better position – but then Fliss whacked my round the ankles and I lost my balance. Fliss, the squishy-poo champ – it was a miracle!

"I won! I won!" she yelped excitedly. "Eat my shorts, losers!"

After a few more rounds of that, and a slap-up pizza dinner from Frankie's dad, it was just starting to get dark. Yay! Even *I* was getting excited now.

We all raced out into the garden, and Frankie promptly grabbed the telescope to look through it first while Lyndz sat at the Mission Control desk, with a pen at the ready.

"What am I meant to be writing down?" she wailed. "Shall I put anything yet?"

"I haven't seen anything yet, dimbo!" Frankie said. "In fact, it's a bit cloudy tonight. Not very good for star-spotting."

It was ages and ages and *ages* before we saw anything. To be honest, it was actually getting a bit boring, looking through the telescope at Cuddington Hill just to see nothing, nothing and *still* nothing!

When it got to nine o'clock and we still hadn't seen anything or written anything down, it was my turn to peer through the telescope. "Maybe we should have another game," I said, putting my eye to the lens. "I mean, this isn't much fun, is it? And it's getting cold."

"Shall I write that down?" Lyndz asked eagerly.

"NO!!" everyone else said.

"Oh, let's look a little bit longer," Frankie begged. "We've got to give it a proper try! Otherwise we'll never know if we really did see something freaky last week!"

"Yeah, but…" I was about to argue, but then I stopped. "Hang on a minute," I muttered. "I think I've spotted something."

I moved the telescope slightly down. There it was again – small green lights in the sky. I blinked. It was definitely there – small green lights hovering in the sky, just around the place we'd seen the lights last week.

"OK, I see something," I said, trying to stay calm. "I'm definitely seeing something – green lights again."

The others all screamed in excitement. "Let me see!" Frankie said, trying to push me off. "Budge up, Rosie!"

"It's not very big," I said, my eye still glued to the lens. "In fact, it looks pretty small. I'm sure it's not half as big as whatever we saw last week. Here, see what you think."

Frankie practically pushed me over in her keenness to get to the telescope.

"Ooh, I see it, I see it!" she said excitedly. "It's moving – it's moving up and down. Now it's on the ground. Ooh – now it's up again. Well spotted, Rosie! Our aliens have returned!"

We all had a look. Fliss was practically hysterical. "I told you 'the plot thickens', didn't I?" she said. "That horoscopes book is AMAZING!!"

"Are we sure it's the same thing we saw last week?" I said doubtfully. "It looks much smaller – and the lights aren't half so bright this time."

"Well, maybe they're shape-changing aliens," Frankie said, waving her hand dismissively. "Maybe they've shrunk themselves so they can sneak around without getting spotted!"

"And maybe they've come back to get your coin – so they're going to sneak in to your house tonight!" Kenny said, eyes gleaming. "Which means only one thing..."

"RUN!!" squealed Lyndz. "Back in the house!"

So, just like last week, the five of us grabbed everything and dashed back into the house at the speed of light.

"Now do you believe it, Rosie?" Frankie asked, her eyes wild with excitement. "Now do you believe that we've seen something freaky?"

I just nodded, feeling dazed. "Yes," I said, with a gulp. "I think I do!"

CHAPTER SEVEN

Well, what can I say? To see flashing lights moving around on Cuddington Hill two weeks on the trot WAS pretty weird, and try as I might, I just couldn't think of a good explanation for it. GULP!!

If it had been difficult to get to sleep last Friday, this week it was a trillion times worse. I'd never seen the others so hysterical with excitement before.

"Why do the aliens keep coming back to Cuddington?" Frankie said eagerly. "Do you think they've been watching us?"

"Why US?" wailed Fliss. "I wish they'd leave us alone!"

"Maybe they've heard about five super-intelligent, gorgeous, funky beings in Cuddington and wanted a closer look," Kenny suggested. "That's us, by the way, in case anyone's wondering!"

"Maybe they want to borrow Fliss's horoscopes book," I said, nudging Kenny.

"Well, only if they're Virgos, I suppose..." Fliss said, taking me seriously as usual.

"I still think they might want their coin back," Lyndz said. "Maybe we should put it back on Cuddington Hill?"

"No way!" screeched Frankie. "That's part of our evidence, Lyndz!"

"I wonder if they're watching us right now?" Kenny said in a creepy voice. "They've probably got all this amazing equipment that lets them see through brick walls from miles away."

"They're probably checking out which of our brains looks the tastiest," I said, playing along. "Wondering which of us to chow down on first!"

Fliss screamed and dived into her sleeping bag head first!

"Oh, YOU don't need to worry!" Frankie said. "They're not interested in a load of fluff and hot air, Mystic!"

"Yeah, there's not enough there to keep even a baby alien alive!" Kenny said, prodding Fliss's sleeping bag with her foot.

Fliss's head shot out again. "I'll have you know that there's nothing wrong with my brain!" she snapped. "And what's more—"

"They're only teasing, Fliss," Lyndz said. "Hey, where's your mystic ball anyway? We can ask it what the aliens are up to!"

Fliss went a bit quiet while she thought. "I *think* I brought it in," she said doubtfully. "I was in such a panic to get inside, I..."

She looked wildly around the room, and then looked stricken. "Oh no, I think I must have left it in your garden, Frankie!"

All five of us looked at each other in silence for a moment. It was really dark outside now, and the thought of creeping around in Frankie's garden in our pyjamas looking for the mystic ball – which was black, anyway, so would be totally invisible out there – did not appeal to anyone.

"Does... er... does anyone fancy going to get it for me?" Fliss said hopefully.

I looked at Kenny. Kenny looked at Frankie. Frankie looked at Lyndz, and Lyndz looked at me.

"No WAY!" all four of us said at the same time.

"Not on your nelly," Frankie said, with a shudder. "I've gone off the idea of meeting an alien suddenly!"

"Oh, pleeeeeease!" Fliss begged. "What if it gets nicked?"

Kenny started to laugh. "Do you really think an alien who's managed to bring a spaceship here from outer space will want to nick a plastic so-called fortune-telling ball?!" she said.

"Well..." Fliss started, then shrugged.

She looked so sorry for herself, I gave her a cuddle. "Come on, then," I sighed. "Let's ALL go. We'll be all right together, won't we?"

"Will we?" Lyndz asked nervously.

"Rosie's right," Kenny said. "Come on! We'll be there and back in two minutes flat if we go now."

So – thanks to Fliss – that's how we all ended up creeping downstairs in our pyjamas and bare feet again.

Frankie grabbed a torch from the kitchen cupboard. "Ready?" she whispered, shining it under her chin, so her whole face went a ghostly yellow.

Fliss gulped, and nodded. "Sorry about this, everyone," she said in a loud whisper. "I didn't mean to—"

"Ssssssshhhhh! You'll wake Mum and Dad up!" Frankie said in a low voice.

"Not to mention letting the aliens know we're about to go outside," Kenny muttered.

Frankie fiddled with the key in the back door and eventually it swung open. Then, just at that moment...

ZAP!

The sky was flooded with light and we saw a huge dazzling flash of lightning right over Cuddington Hill. Just for a second, it was as bright as daylight. Then it went pitch black again, and there was a loud rumbling thunderclap which made us all jump out of our skins.

Frankie slammed the door shut again, and locked it, quick as quick. Her fingers were shaking as she did so.

"Er... I've changed my mind," she said. "Let's go back to my room – quick!"

We all charged back upstairs gratefully as the rain started pelting down outside.

"Wasn't that spooky?" Kenny said, once we were back in Frankie's bedroom. She ran over to the window and peered out. "Just look at it! There goes the lightning again!"

ZAP!

Fliss clapped her hands over her ears. She gets a bit nervous in thunderstorms. "Do you think the aliens have caused it?" she asked anxiously.

"Maybe," Frankie said, wrinkling her forehead as she thought. "Maybe there's lots of extra electricity whizzing round in the air from their spaceship – and it caused the lightning to strike in that very spot!"

"Oh, I bet you're right!" Fliss said, her eyes wide.

"I wonder if the aliens got blasted by it?" Lyndz said thoughtfully.

"We're gonna HAVE to go back up the hill," Kenny said. "This is all too freaky to be true."

I said nothing. I still wasn't sure the thunderstorm was connected to the lights we'd seen. But one thing was for sure – much as I hated to admit it, Fliss's horoscope book had been right again. The plot was *definitely* thickening now!

The next day, Fliss went charging out into the garden before she'd even had her breakfast. She was dead worried that her step-dad would be cross if she had lost her new present straight away – and more importantly, there were lots of questions she wanted to ask the mystic ball about last night!

When she came back inside, she was all smiles again. "It's quite dry!" she said happily. "It had rolled under a bush – look!"

"Now, if you were a real mystic, you'd have known that, of course," Kenny pointed out, but Fliss was just so relieved to have her ball back, she didn't care.

"Is Kenny going to get on my nerves all day?" she asked the ball, smiling sweetly

84

across the table at Kenny. She tipped it over. "'No'. Oh, good, that'll make a nice change!" she said.

I caught Lyndz's eye and we both giggled. Kenny, for once, had no comeback. One-nil to Fliss!

We all ate our breakfasts mega-quickly so we could go exploring on the hill again. This time, Fliss went just as fast as the rest of us on our bikes as we pedalled furiously through Frankie's estate to get there. The night before all seemed too weird to be true, now it was daylight again. The flashing lights, and then that crashing thunderstorm that had come from out of nowhere... Freaky! I just couldn't work the whole thing out.

Once we got to the top, the five of us charged about like mad things. Lyndz was convinced that one area of grass was looking especially flat that day. "As if something really big had landed on it," she mused.

"Or the wind's been blowing it, maybe?" I said sarcastically, and she went a bit red.

"Mmm, maybe," she said, sounding disappointed.

We didn't find any more scorch marks, although we must have looked at almost every blade of grass up there. We didn't find any more strange green discs either. And there wasn't even a sighting of the M&Ms to give us a bit of a laugh. But we did find...

"Hey, look at this!"

It was eagle-eyed Kenny who spotted it. She was holding up something silver with a triumphant look on her face. "Come and look!" she yelled.

I felt my heart start pounding. What now?

But as soon as I'd had a closer look, I wasn't so excited.

"That's just a tag from someone's key-ring that's broken off," I said, handing it back to Kenny. "It's not anything alien – definitely not!"

The others were about to trudge off in disappointment, when Fliss grabbed it off Kenny.

"Hang on a minute, I recognise this," she said, staring at it intently. "I definitely recognise this. I've seen someone who has a key-ring just like this."

We all stared at it again. It was a silver oval

shape with a picture of a racing car on it.

"Loads of people must have one of those," I said dismissively. It was only an old broken bit of key-ring, after all!

"I know whose it is!" Lyndz said suddenly. "It's Dave's, isn't it? Caretaker Dave from school!"

"Yes!" squealed Fliss. "That's it. I KNEW I'd seen it somewhere before!"

"Yeah, he got it on holiday in Italy, didn't he?" Frankie said. "Turn it over, Kenz, what's on the other side?"

Kenny flipped the tag over. ITALIA, it said on the back.

We all stared at each other.

"It's definitely Dave's, then," I said, slowly. "Not many people in Cuddington have silver Italian key-rings, do they?"

"So what was Dave doing up here when he lost it?" Lyndz pondered.

Frankie's eyes went wide. "You don't think he... No," she said slowly. "He couldn't have been."

"WHAT?!" the rest of us yelled.

"You don't think he's been kidnapped by the

aliens, do you?" she asked, sounding horrified at the thought.

There was this terrible silence.

"Surely not," I said in the end, trying to sound confident. Inside my tummy, a hundred butterflies were going crazy. This was all getting far too creepy for my liking.

"But I really like Dave!" Fliss said, sounding on the verge of tears. "Why would they want to take Dave?"

"Yeah, why couldn't they take the M&Ms?" muttered Kenny. "The world would be a far better place without them!"

"Maybe his key-ring got broken when he put up a struggle," Lyndz said. "Oh no! I can't believe they've got him!"

"Hang on, hang on," I said, trying to sound calm, even though I was feeling as frightened as they were. "We don't know if he's been kidnapped for sure. Let's wait and see if he's at school when we go back on Monday. I mean, he could have just been walking his dog up here when his key-ring got broken and fell out of his pocket."

"Rosie's right," Fliss said in a wobbly voice.

"No point getting scared until Monday. And then we can all be terrified!"

"And if Dave HASN'T been kidnapped, maybe he knows something we don't," Frankie pointed out. "Maybe he saw the whole thing! Whatever, let's go straight round to that caretaker's shed on Monday morning to find out just what is going on!"

CHAPTER EIGHT

Normally I absolutely *hate* the first day back at school after the summer holidays. Is it the pits or WHAT? It's got to be one of the worst days of the year, if you ask me. But then, my mum thinks it's one of the BEST days of the year because she can chill out when we're back at school again. "Peace and quiet day" she calls it.

This year, going back to school felt a bit weird, though. Part of me was gutted about the thought of school work and tests and wearing school uniform, as usual. But part of me, for the first time ever, felt excited and a teeny bit scared. What if we went to assembly and Mrs Poole, our head teacher, told us that Dave wouldn't be our caretaker this year because he'd mysteriously disappeared at the weekend? Can you imagine?! I think Fliss would scream the school down in shock.

Anyway, SOMETHING was going on with Dave, we were convinced of it. He had to have some connection with the whole saga – and he was our best hope yet of finding out what was going on. I wanted to know all about it – we *all* did!

"You're in a funny mood today," Mum said as we had breakfast that morning.

I put down my spoon. "Am I?" I said innocently.

"Yes," she said, puffing hard on her cigarette. "You're very quiet. Anything I should know about?"

"No," I said, and started eating my cereal again.

"She's got a boyfriend," Adam said, kicking me under the table.

"No, I have not!" I said indignantly. Trust Darth Vader to stick his oar in!

"You have, I heard you talking to Frankie on

the phone about him." Adam was smirking his head off. He loves winding me up! "Dave, isn't it?"

"Ooh, dishy Dave, eh?" said Tiffany, putting on her make-up and earwigging as usual. She's the biggest gossip in Cuddington, after Fliss's mum. "When do we get to meet him, then?"

"Oh, shurrup, you two," I growled. You wouldn't think they're both older than me when they act like five-year-olds, would you?

Even Mum was getting interested now. "Is that true, Rosie? You are a dark horse! Have you really got a boyfriend?"

"No!" I practically yelled. "Dave is the school caretaker if you're that interested! And he is NOT my boyfriend!"

"Ooh, the older man! I see," Tiffany muttered, combing her hair in front of the mirror.

I glared at her but she was too interested in her own reflection to notice.

"So why did you keep going on about this Dave to Frankie, then?" Adam wanted to know.

"I..." I started – and then stopped again. If I said anything at all about aliens, I knew my whole family would fall about laughing. "Why do you have to be so nosey all the time?" I snapped at him.

"All right, that's enough bickering!" Mum said in a warning voice. "This is my peace and quiet day, remember? Now eat your cereal before it goes to mush!"

I gobbled down my breakfast, cleaned my teeth and ran off to school before I had to face any more embarrassing questions about Dave. It was bad enough them thinking that he was my BOYFRIEND, but if I so much as *mentioned* that we thought Dave had been kidnapped by aliens... well, I'd never have heard the end of it. I know I'm a cynic, but the rest of my family beat me hands down!

I met up with the others outside the school gates. Kenny was looking uncomfortable in her school uniform and kept tugging at the collar of her school blouse. "I'm sure this never used to be so itchy," she moaned. "Give me a pair of shorts and a T-shirt any day!"

"Do you know what? I asked the magic ball if this was going to be a good day today and it said 'No'," Fliss said anxiously. "I don't like the sound of that, do you? Mind you, last night I asked if the aliens were going to come and get me and it said yes to that – and I lay awake all night and they didn't!"

"Maybe the ball got a bit of water in it the other night at Frankie's," Lyndz suggested. "That might have made it go a bit funny."

"Or maybe it's just a cheap plastic toy with no magical powers at all?" Kenny said in a low voice. I think she was saying it to me rather than Fliss, but Fliss gave her the most horrible look so I think she heard every word.

"So it's Operation Dave this morning," Frankie announced as we walked up towards school. "Dave is the key to solving this mystery, so everyone keep their eyes peeled for sightings of our target. If we spot him – we confront him with the key-ring. And if we DON'T spot him, then..."

"Then what?" Lyndz prompted eagerly.

"Then... I don't know yet," Frankie confessed. "But remember, the Sleepover Club isn't afraid of anything!"

"Except aliens," Fliss said, looking a bit sick. "I'm very afraid of them!"

"And insects," I pointed out. "And ghost stories. And…"

"Thanks, Rosie," she said, glaring at me. "You're making me feel really brave, you know!"

Oops! At this rate, *everyone* was going to be in Fliss's bad books before school had even started!

When we got to the playground, all five of us were looking round eagerly, hoping to spot Dave. As time went on without a single sighting of him, Frankie started to get more and more excited.

"I knew it!" she was saying. "I knew it! He's gone! The moment I saw his key-ring up there, I knew something fishy was…"

Then Frankie's voice trailed away to nothing and we all turned to see what she was looking at.

"Oh," she said.

"It's Dave!" Fliss hissed, as we all spotted him at the same time. "So what now? Do we confront him?"

"Bagsy not me confronting him!" Lyndz said at once.

"Me neither!" said Fliss, looking horrified at the thought.

"There's something... different about him," Kenny said, screwing her eyes up as she stared at him. "He doesn't look the same somehow, does he?"

We all peered at Dave, who was emptying the litter bin in the playground.

"What do you mean, different?" I asked. He looked the same as ever to me. Tall, unbrushed hair, jeans, checked shirt... yep, that was Dave all right.

Frankie suddenly clutched my arm. "What if the aliens have taken over Dave's body?" she said dramatically. "He'd look a bit different then, wouldn't he?"

"Come on, he doesn't look THAT different!" I protested.

"Now you mention it, there *is* something funny about him," Lyndz said. "I think it's that expression on his face. He does look pretty weird, actually."

"So would you if you'd been taken over by an alien!" Fliss said, with a head-to-toe shudder.

Just then, Dave turned and caught sight of the five of us looking at him. He waved and smiled, and I suddenly felt sick with nerves. I was sure Frankie couldn't be right, but what if something HAD happened to Dave up on Cuddington Hill the other night?

"He's coming over!" squeaked Lyndz frantically. "What are we going to do? What are we going to SAY?"

"We're going to face the music," Frankie said firmly. "Try and act normal. Just try and act normal!"

Act normal? I was feeling terrified. And one look at the others told me they felt the same way!

We all held our breath as he walked across the playground towards us. For all Frankie's brave words, she was looking as sick as the rest of us.

"Hi, you lot!" Dave called. "Good holidays?"

I couldn't say a word. I just couldn't take my eyes off his face, wondering if that was really Dave the caretaker, or...

"Er... er... mmmm," stammered Frankie.

"Good result on Saturday for City, wasn't

it?" he said, turning to Kenny. His eyes seemed a really bright green in the sun.

Kenny gulped, blinked and then...

"Aaargh!" she screamed loudly, and charged off into the distance. And then, one by one, we all charged after her, leaving Dave standing there on his own.

"Did you see the way he looked at me?" Kenny gasped once we'd caught up with her. "His eyes looked all glassy – and I swear they've changed colour! They never used to be green, did they?"

My heart was thudding away inside me. I tried to be calm myself down – I mean, I *was* supposed to be the rational one, after all!

"Look, Dave is probably just the same nice Dave he's always been," I said. "Except now he must be thinking we've all completely lost the plot! Let's think about it for a minute. Just because we found his key-ring on Cuddington Hill doesn't mean ANYTHING, right? It doesn't prove there's any connection between him and those lights we saw, does it?"

There was a silence. No-one was looking at me.

"Right?!" I said, a bit louder this time.

"I know what I saw," Kenny said stubbornly. "Alien eyes, looking out from Dave's face. Bright green alien eyes. That's what I saw!"

"Remember ages ago when we were trying to matchmake Dave and Brown Owl, when we decided that Dave looks like Brad Pitt?" Frankie said suddenly.

We all nodded, remembering.

"Well, Brad Pitt has blue eyes, doesn't he?" Frankie said. She practically shouted it, she was so worked up. "And so did Dave – until today!"

With a sickening lurch, I had to admit she was right. "Which means that..." I began, not wanting it to be true.

"*He's an alien!*" Fliss and Lyndz both screamed at the same time, clutching each other in fright. "AAAAARGHHHH!"

CHAPTER NINE

I was starting to get *totally* freaked out by all of this. The green alien eyes were the last straw. People's eyes didn't just change overnight, did they? Not unless something really weird had happened to them!

As we walked into the classroom, I heard two familiar – and horrible – voices. The M&Ms! Ugh, just who I LEAST wanted to see right then! How sad that THEY hadn't been kidnapped by the aliens. Mind you, they were probably too disgusting, even by alien standards!

"Oh, look, if it isn't the lovely Pullover Club," said Emily yucky Berryman. "Or whatever it is they call themselves."

"Pushover Club, more like!" sniggered Emma Goblin-face Hughes. "Ha ha!"

"You'll be the Fall-Over Club if you don't watch it!" I said, sticking my tongue out at them.

"Yeah? Well we still haven't forgotten about your little waterworks display the other week," Emma said. "So I think it's you five that might just find yourself in a nasty little accident!"

"Or a nasty BIG accident!" sniggered Emily, giving us a mean look.

"Oh dear, how we've missed your dazzling wit," Kenny said sarcastically. "It's great to see you two again, though. Makes me feel *soooo* much better about myself!"

"Yes, I always feel particularly beautiful when I'm in the same room as the M&Ms!" Frankie added. "Not to mention particularly intelligent!"

The M&Ms looked cross at that. "Yeah, well..." Emily started – but that was all she managed to say.

"Settle down, everyone!" called Mrs Weaver,

our teacher. "Quiet, please! I hope you all had a nice summer holiday – I'd just like to remind you that this is actually a classroom and you're back at school now, where *I* do the talking!"

We all went quiet. Mrs Weaver is the sort of teacher you don't muck about with. Even Kenny gets a bit scared of her if she's in a bad temper!

"That's better," she smiled. "Welcome back. This morning we're going to start off with our new topic for the term, which is all about weather. I'm going to split you into groups and I want each group to find out more about a certain type of weather for a new display on the wall."

"Can we do thunderstorms?" Kenny said at once, her hand shooting up in the air.

Mrs Weaver smiled. "Nice to have such an enthusiastic group over there!" she said. "Yes, certainly. The other groups will be..."

Drone, drone, drone. I'd switched off my brain already. The other groups could have been finding out about fairies and Father Christmas for all I knew! I made the thumbs-up sign to Kenny and winked. Quick thinking from Mcklali, there!!

Lyndz rushed over and grabbed one of the encyclopaedias as soon as Mrs Weaver had sorted all the groups out. This was very handy! Using a school morning to find out more about that freaky thunderstorm!

"My granny used to say that thunderstorms were the noise of the gods playing marbles in the sky," Fliss said importantly.

Frankie gave her a withering look. "All grannies say things like that," she said. "Grannies live in a world of their own, half the time!"

"Thunderstorms happen when it's been really hot," I said. "I remember Tiffany doing a project about it at school. Something to do with lots of pressure in the air, or... Oh, I dunno! Anyway, what I'm trying to say is that it was dead hot and muggy on Friday, wasn't it? So it was probably that which caused the storm."

"Yeah, but it was so freaky, the way that lightning struck the very second we opened Frankie's back door," Lyndz argued. "Almost as if something knew we were there, and was trying to frighten us..."

"Maybe the aliens were trying to stop us getting my magic ball!" Fliss suggested, with a shiver. "Maybe..."

"Give us that, Lyndz," I said, grabbing the book off her. Anything to stop Fliss getting carried away! "OK, let's see what it says about lightning... Here we are. 'Lightning – A flash of light in the sky, during a thunderstorm'."

"We know *that*!" Kenny said impatiently.

"Give me a chance!" I said. "There's more. 'Caused by a burst of electricity, either between clouds or between a cloud and the Earth'."

"Or by the Earth and a spaceship, of course!" Frankie said solemnly.

The others nodded in agreement. "Just as we thought," said Kenny in a hushed voice. "We HAVE to tackle Dave about this. It all adds up!"

"I hope the aliens didn't get hurt by the lightning," Lyndz said anxiously. "It was a HUGE bolt, wasn't it?"

I burst out laughing. "Trust you, Lyndz!

Quick – someone tell Rolf Harris to take them to ALIEN Hospital!"

Fliss got out her horoscopes book. "Well, my stars for today say that I have to 'check the facts'," she said. "As usual, it's right! But how are we going to do that?"

"We can't just accuse Dave outright," Frankie said. "If the aliens know we've got wind of them, *we'll* be the next ones to get body-snatched!"

"We'll have to spy on him, follow him around," I said. "See if he's up to anything strange. Frankie's right – we don't want to accuse him. I'm sure he isn't, but if he really *is* an alien, then…"

"He could zap us on the spot," Kenny said cheerfully. "How was YOUR first day at school? Oh, you know, zapped by an alien, the usual…"

"Quiet, everyone!" called Mrs Weaver. "It's break time now. We'll carry on with this afterwards."

"Perfect timing," Frankie said. "Time for Sleepover Club to go undercover and 'check our facts'!"

* * *

It's got to be said – as a team, we're pretty good at finding things out. If you've heard about any of our other adventures, I'm sure you'll agree! Five brains are much better than one at solving mysteries – but even by our standards, this was proving a difficult nut to crack!

Lyndz suggested looking through the window of Dave's tool shed to see if we could spot anything strange. "WYou never know we might see another of those green discs, or see him communicating with the spaceship!" she said excitedly.

"What if everything's perfectly normal in there?" I said. "Should we go in and speak to him?"

"Oh, do we have to?" Fliss whimpered. "I don't want to get eaten alive!"

"Silly!" I said, nudging her. "We'll just ask him what he's been doing on Cuddington Hill, that's all. We can tell him we found his key-ring up there."

"Yeah, and if he's feeling guilty, I bet his face will be a picture!" Kenny said. "That'll totally give the game away!"

"Are we ready and steady?" Frankie asked. "Then let's go, gadgets, go!"

I felt a bit nervous as we approached Dave's tool shed. Nearly all of the weird things that had been happening could be explained away quite easily – but it still didn't make me feel any better. I just had this nagging feeling that something wasn't quite right.

Once we were near the shed, Kenny put her finger to her lips. The rest of us waited a couple of metres away while she crept up to the shed and peeped through the window. Then she turned back and beckoned us over, her eyes shining.

My heart started pounding. What had she seen?

Me, Fliss, Frankie and Lyndz crept up beside her and she pointed through the window with a shaking hand.

There sat Dave at a table, working on something... *something with a flashing green light on it*!

My jaw dropped. I just couldn't believe it. I stared at the others open-mouthed, not knowing what to say. Until now, I'd had an answer for everything – or almost everything. The lightning was just a storm, the key-ring hadn't proved anything, but now... now the evidence was staring us right in the face. Dave – or whoever he was – was mending part of the spaceship!

"Oh my goodness, I don't believe it!" Fliss said in a loud voice – so loud, that Dave turned round to see who was outside.

"Fliss, you idiot!" Frankie said. "Don't give the game away!"

"We've got to tell someone about this," Lyndz said urgently, her teeth chattering with fear. "Quick! Where's Mrs Weaver?"

Just then, the door of the shed opened. Dave!

"What are you lot up to, sneaking around here?" he said.

Seeing those bright green eyes again gave me goosepimples all over.

"N-n-n-nothing," I stammered. "Gotta go! Bye!"

"Look, there's Mrs Weaver!" shouted Kenny. "Quick, run!"

The five of us started to leg it towards her. "What's going on?" shouted Dave after us. *"What the heck's going on?"*

CHAPTER TEN

Thank goodness Mrs Weaver was on playground duty that day! The five of us pelted down towards her. I was feeling very frightened now. I'd never really believed in aliens before – but now I did, and I was very *very* scared of them!

"Girls! What on earth's the matter?" Mrs Weaver said as we charged towards her. "Is one of you hurt?"

"No, it's D-D-D-Dave!" Frankie said, stumbling over the word.

"What, Dave's hurt?" Mrs Weaver said. "Well, the speed he's running, he looks all right to me!"

"No, you don't understand," Kenny said urgently. "He's…"

"I'm what?" Dave said, as he caught up with us. "What is this all about? Why do you five keep screaming and running away every time you see me?"

"Must be those new contact lenses!" Mrs Weaver said to him teasingly. "Driving the girls wild, obviously!"

The five of us looked at each other. "Colour contact lenses, is that what he told you?" Frankie said disbelievingly. "Yeah, *right*!"

"What?!" Dave asked, sounding confused. "What do you mean?"

"We found this," Kenny said accusingly, holding the silver key tag out in front of him. "On Cuddington Hill." She raised her eyebrows meaningfully at him.

He took it from her. "Excellent! I wondered what had happened to that," he said, putting it in his pocket. "Thanks, girls – but you could have just given it to me in the first place, instead of this pantomime!"

"Is that it?" Mrs Weaver said. "Is that what all the fuss was about?"

"Not on your nelly!" Frankie said indignantly. "We haven't even got started yet!"

"He's an alien!" Fliss shouted, unable to hold back any more. "We saw him with Frankie's telescope – there were flashing lights up on Cuddington Hill, and then we found an alien coin, and..."

"And then there was this huge storm, caused by the spaceship!" Lyndz added. "And then we found Dave's key-ring!"

"*And* his eyes have turned green!" I said, pointing at them.

"AND we've just seen him mending the spaceship!" Kenny said, folding her arms across her chest. "Don't even *try* to deny it!"

I gulped as a strange expression came over Dave's face. What would he do, now the truth was out? Would he zap us? Turn us into aliens, too?

No – he started to laugh! A great big roaring laugh! He laughed so hard that he couldn't speak for a minute.

Mrs Weaver was looking totally baffled by it all. "Will someone please tell me what this is all about?" she asked. "Is it some sort of joke?"

Dave shook his head and managed to stop laughing. "That is the best yet!" he said. He practically had tears in his eyes from all the laughing. "What will you lot think of next?" he said.

I bit my lip. Uh-oh... Either Dave was doing a brilliant bluff, or the Sleepover Club might have made a bit of a boo-boo this time...

Kenny wasn't having any of it, though. "How do you explain that bit of the spaceship we saw you fixing in your shed, then?" she asked. "Let's hear it!"

"Certainly!" Dave said, grinning. "If you'd like to accompany me back to the shed, I'll show you exactly what I was fixing – and I'm sorry to say, it wasn't a spaceship!"

I was starting to feel a bit silly. Green eyes or not, it seemed that Dave wasn't really an alien, after all. We had just made ourselves look complete idiots – and to make it even worse, the M&Ms were listening in and they'd heard every word of it!

We traipsed back to the shed with Dave. Frankie, Kenny and Fliss still seemed convinced of the alien plot but one look at

Lyndz told me she was starting to have second thoughts too.

Then I heard a voice from behind. "Fancy still believing in aliens at their age!" it said. "What a bunch of babies!"

"Talk about stupid!" came another voice. The M&Ms of course. They were just loving this!

When we got to his shed, Dave pulled the door open. "There!" he said. "That's your spaceship! Not so scary now, is it?"

There on his desk sat an innocent-looking remote-controlled helicopter. And there on its top and tail were a couple of – you guessed it – green flashing lights.

"I don't believe it!" groaned Kenny. "That's our spaceship?"

"I reckon," Dave said. "Good, isn't she? I normally fly her in the day, but decided to fit a few lights on it so I could take her out for a night flight."

"Right," said Frankie wearily. "And we thought..."

There was a great cackle from the M&Ms who looked as if they were about to wet themselves, clutching at each other in fits of giggles.

"I had to pack up and go fairly early on Friday because of that awful storm," Dave continued. "Shame, 'cos I'd only just fitted the lights on and it seemed a pity to go home early on her first night flight and all. Still." He grinned at us. "Maybe next weekend, I'll be able to put on a longer show for you, eh?"

The M&Ms gave another scream of laughter, which was our cue to get out of there – as fast as we could!

"Sorry we thought you were an alien," Lyndz said, almost in a whisper.

"I'm glad you're not," Kenny said, adding as an afterthought, "I suppose."

"Well, I'm not glad," Frankie said, once Dave was out of earshot. "I'm totally gutted!"

"My horoscope DID say for us to check our facts," Fliss sighed. "That must have been what it meant. See? I told you my stars are never wrong!"

Kenny promptly tripped her up and she went flying on the grass.

"What did you do that for?" she shouted.

"Your stars didn't tell you THAT was going to happen, did they?" growled Kenny.

There was a bit of a bad feeling in the air. I think we were all really disappointed that the 'spaceship' had turned out to be a false alarm. And even worse, that the M&Ms had found out all about it, and knew what total idiots we'd been!

"We're never going to live this down!" I groaned, hearing them singing the theme from *Star Wars* behind us. "Oh, they're just loving this, listen to them!"

"Feel the force, Sleepover Club!" Emma shouted. "Feel the force – and feel the embarrassment!"

"Ignore them," Lyndz said through gritted teeth. "Pretend we can't hear them!"

But it was too late. Kenny had turned and started doing her 'Concorde' at them – where she put her arms out to the sides, screamed her loudest scream and ran at them, full pelt.

The M&Ms went from looking smug to terrified and immediately pegged it away from her. They know what Kenny's capable of when she's in a bad mood!

Two minutes later, Kenny was back, having seen them off. "That's got rid of those two morons!" she said, looking a bit happier.

Just then, Frankie stopped dead in her tracks. "Hang on a minute!" she said. "What was it Dave said? He took his helicopter out for the *first* time on Friday night, which means that..."

We all stared at her.

"Which means that it can't have been the helicopter we saw the week before," Kenny said slowly.

"Yes!" Frankie said excitedly. "So what did we see at first? Only the *second* lot of flashing green lights were Dave's helicopter."

"We did say it looked smaller on Friday, didn't we?" Lyndz said.

Fliss's mouth quivered. "Oh, no you don't!" she said. "We've just proved Dave isn't an alien, and it was just his helicopter we saw. Don't start making out we saw a spaceship again, *pleeeeease!*"

"Fliss is right," I said. "It was fun to think we'd seen a UFO for a while, but let's face it – it was probably just someone else's remote-controlled plane we saw the first time. Let's not go down that road again."

Kenny nodded. "Yeah, I agree," she said. "Sorry, Frank – maybe we've just been watching too many scary TV programmes lately."

Frankie shook her head stubbornly. "No way! I know there was something weird about it! The scorch marks on the grass, and that green disc..."

"Yeah, what happened to that, anyway?" Lyndz asked. "I'd forgotten all about it!"

"Safe and sound in my purse as always," Frankie said, digging it out of her pocket. "Here."

As she took it out, all five of us gasped at the exact same time. As she tilted it up to the light, there seemed to be a hologram of a creature on one side. And as she moved it back and forwards, I swear the creature started waving to us...

Well, your guess is as good as mine on that one. All I can tell you is that the disc definitely *didn't* have that hologram on it when we found it. No way! One of us would have seen it, without a doubt. So was it a trick of the light? No. The hologram was on the disc all day – and then the next day, it vanished again, just like that. Every now and then, when we're at Frankie's, one of us will get it out and fiddle with it, trying to see the waving creature again – but we've never seen it since.

Now that IS weird. Frankie, Kenny and Lyndz all swear it was a message from outer space. They're totally convinced all over again that we saw a spaceship that first time, although we've never seen anything except stars through the telescope since then. Fliss doesn't really want to know. It's scared her witless and she'd rather not think about it. Fair enough!

What was that? What do *I* think about it? Well, I really don't know. And maybe I'll never know! Do you have any ideas?

I'll tell you one thing, though. I've been reading up on space, and the sky is a big old place, you know. There are billions and zillions of galaxies and star systems all floating about out there. Surely our tiny little Earth isn't the only planet to have living creatures on it?

I'll leave you to chew over that one. It's keeping me awake at night, I can tell you. This is Rosie Maria Carromi Cartwright signing off. Sweet dreams!

Sleepover Club Vampires

An imprint of HarperCollinsPublishers

CHAPTER ONE

Brilliant! It's you! I've been looking everywhere for you. How's it going? Or should I say "Hoots mon! Och aye the noo! And 'Donald where's yer troosers'!" Hey, hey, hey – you're thinking that old Kenny's finally lost it, aren't you? Go on admit it! Well you're wrong, so very wrong. All I'm trying to do is set the scene a bit, you know, get you in the mood for our latest Sleepover adventure.

Whadayamean, it sounds like the weirdest adventure yet if we all end up talking gibberish in a strange accent? That was a *Scottish* accent, dummy, and I am half-Scottish so I should know what I'm talking about.

I know the others wanted to see you first so they could spill the beans. Frankie *always* thinks that she should be the storyteller, just because she fancies herself as a bit of an actress. And Fliss, well, I know that she wanted to tell you about it, because she says that only she can begin to describe how scary it really was. (That's just because she's a big scaredy-cat herself. You should have seen her this time. Talk about quivering mess!) Rosie was pretty carried away by the adventure too, she was so glad that her mum had let her come. But I guess if anyone other than *moi* was going to tell you the story, it should be Lyndz. You see, it's kind of because of her that it happened in the first place.

Now I don't know about you, but I think that autumn half-term is often a major letdown. The weather's usually wet and windy, so you can't spend too much time outdoors. The nights are drawing in so your parents start panicking about you being home early. Summer's so far away you can barely remember it, and Christmas is just a bit of a twinkle in the distance. And basically you're kind of stuck in the middle.

I can't ever remember going away during autumn half-term before, but this year Dad asked us one night over dinner:

" How does a week in Scotland grab you?"

"Ooh I know this one, don't help me!" I piped up. "Is the answer something like 'under your kilt'?"

Mum, Dad, my oldest sister Emma and my yuckiest sister Molly, all stared at me with open mouths. (Molly's was still full of mashed potato so it wasn't a pretty sight!)

"No Kenny," said Dad at last. "This isn't a joke. We've decided that this year we're going to spend a few days with Great Uncle Bob."

I could tell by Mum's face that it was more a case of *Dad* deciding that we were going, there was no *we* about it.

We'd often talked about going to stay with Great Uncle Bob in the past, but Mum had always come up with a million and one reasons why we couldn't. Whenever I asked her what Great Uncle Bob was like, she thought for about half an hour, her face becoming more and more agitated, before finally saying something like, "He's very eccentric," through gritted teeth.

"It'll be great fun!" Dad reassured us, trying his best to ignore Mum's black looks. "We'll be there for Bob's annual party. It's a real treat by all accounts."

"Is it his birthday or something?" Molly asked, all shiny-eyed with enthusiasm (puke!).

"No, it's a tradition he started some years ago," Dad explained. "On the last Saturday in October, he invites everyone from the next village to join him for a massive shindig before winter sets in."

"Cool!" Molly gushed.

My sister's enthusiasm just about made me want to throw up. It's not that I'm a misery guts or anything. In fact there's usually no one who enjoys a good party more than me. It's just that I was kind of worried about someone and I knew that it wouldn't exactly be fiesta-time in their household over half-term.

You're not going to believe it when I tell you that the person I was worried about was Lyndz. Yes Lyndz, our Lyndz, Sleepover Lyndz! I knew you'd be shocked. She's just about the happiest person around, isn't she? Normally. But things weren't normal at Lyndz's place any more. You see, her mum was being a bit – well, weird, basically.

Now you know Lyndz's mum, don't you? Isn't she just about the most laid-back person on the planet? I mean, my mum has always said she doesn't know how Mrs Collins copes with bringing up *five* children. (Yep, Lyndz has *four* brothers, two older than she is and two younger.)

Not only that, but Mrs Collins also works, running a class teaching women how to have babies. She helps out at the local playgroup too. Lyndz's house is always in a mess – part of it is either being pulled down or built up. Mrs Collins just takes it all in her stride and bakes cakes and stuff even though the roof's falling down around her ears. And when we have sleepovers at

Lyndz's, she's really cool because she says she loves having girls around the place.

"You make a nice change from those great smelly sons of mine!" she smiles. And she doesn't bat an eyelid when we get up to some of our silly stunts.

Well that's what Mrs Collins *used* to be like. For the last few weeks she's been really different. She looks kind of grey and tired all the time, she hardly ever laughs and she just seems kind of fed up with everything.

"What's up with your mum?" we asked Lyndz the last time we were over there for a sleepover. "She seems a bit down today."

"Today!" Lyndz snorted. "She's down *every* day. I can't remember her ever being up!"

The rest of us looked at each other and pulled worried faces.

"But your mum always used to be so bubbly," Frankie reminded her. "Maybe something's happened to upset her."

"Well, I think she's kind of upset that we're not going to our grandparents in Holland at half-term," Lyndz confided. "She'd really been looking forward to it, then we had to cancel it. I think it was probably because it was going to cost too much money. I heard her and Dad arguing about it."

"Oh dear!" we all clucked sympathetically.

"But I can't believe she's still upset about that," Lyndz mumbled. "She's known for weeks that we couldn't go."

"Maybe she's really ill," Fliss suggested. "She doesn't look too great, does she?"

"Fliss!" we yelled together, piling on top of her to shut her up.

"Gerroff!" Fliss spluttered. "I was only saying…"

"Well, don't!" Rosie giggled, twanging one of the scrunchies in Fliss's hair and mussing up her beautiful blonde plaits.

"You're going to pay for that!" shrieked Fliss and chased us out of Lyndz's room, down the stairs and through the lounge.

"Chase, chase, chase!" yelled Ben, Lyndz's four-year-old brother, tagging along behind us.

We ran out into the hall – but didn't realise until it was too late that a load of plywood had been stacked against one wall. It was dark so we couldn't see too well, and the first thing we knew about it was when we tripped over it. It came shooting down all over us and all over the floor. It made such a loud CRACK that Ben started to howl from shock.

"WHAT IS GOING ON HERE?" a voice boomed from behind us. "Lyndsey Collins, I thought you had more sense, I really did."

Lyndz's mum appeared with a face as black as thunder. She scooped Ben into her arms and just stood there ranting at us with her hair all over the place.

"I have enough to deal with without extra chaos brought about by you lot. Now you know the rules, Lyndz – stay in your room and don't go chasing about all over the house. Mind you, if your father ever finishes sorting out this hallway it will be a miracle. All my married life I've lived in a mess, and I'm just about sick of it. Now go upstairs and play quietly. I'll call you when supper's ready!"

She stalked back into the kitchen and we slunk up to Lyndz's room.

Nobody said a word until we were safely upstairs. Then we all sank down on Lyndz's bed.

"Crikey Lyndz, I see what you mean!" Frankie gasped.

"Yeah, I mean that sounded more like Fliss's mum than yours!" I agreed. "Has she been taking lessons from her?"

Fliss looked as though she was about to have a go at me. Then she noticed the big fat tears trickling down Lyndz's cheeks.

"Never mind," she soothed, putting an arm around Lyndz's shoulders. "Your mum's probably just having a bit of a bad time at the moment. You know, sometimes stuff seems to get on top of mothers, doesn't it? It'll pass, I'm sure."

We all nodded, although you could tell that really we weren't sure at all.

"Well I hope it's passed before half-term," Lyndz sniffed. "Because it's not going to be a barrel of laughs with Mum like this, is it?"

We all had to agree with that.

And I just couldn't get that thought out of my head as Dad was telling us about Great

Uncle Bob's marvellous party. I just wished there was some way that I could cheer up Lyndz. And her mum.

CHAPTER TWO

When I got to school the next day, Frankie was in the middle of a kickboxing frenzy. I had to dive out of her way pretty sharpish otherwise I'd have had my teeth kicked out.

"Hey Buffy, slow down there! I'm not a vampire that needs slaying, you know!" I grinned, leaping on to her back. We've been best friends forever, me and Frankie. The Sleepover Club kind of came along later. It was at times like this that I felt like we were about four again!

"Ha-*ya*!" She flung me on to the ground.

"How do I know that? Appearances can be deceptive!"

"Well I haven't got pointy teeth for a start…"

"That's a matter of opinion!" grinned Rosie.

"… and blood is definitely *not* my drink of choice!" I continued. "I much prefer Dr Pepper!"

"Aha! You mean you enjoy quaffing a medico's vital juices!" Frankie hovered over me menacingly. "Interesting!"

"Hey Lyndz, Fliss, help me out, would you?" I called over to them. "Buffy here's gone into overdrive!"

But neither Lyndz nor Fliss moved. They carried on leaning against the wall. We could tell just by looking at their faces that something was seriously wrong.

"Wassup?" Frankie, Rosie and I raced over to them.

Lyndz just shook her head and started to sob.

"It's Lyndz's mum," Fliss told us quietly. "She went ballistic again last night, then started to cry and couldn't stop. She said she didn't know why she was so upset, she just felt miserable."

"Is she OK today?" Rosie asked sympathetically.

"She said she was going to go and have a chat with a friend," Fliss continued, not giving Lyndz the chance to reply. "I think that should make her feel better, don't you?"

"Oh yeah!" Frankie nodded. "My gran always says, 'a problem shared is a problem halved'. She'll probably be feeling much better by tonight Lyndz, you'll see."

"I hope so," Lyndz sniffed. She looked so miserable.

We all gave her a big hug, and for the rest of the day we made sure that we did whatever Lyndz wanted. If she was having a rough time at home, the least we could do was cheer her up at school.

I know that as the afternoon wore on, Lyndz started to feel pretty churned up at the thought of going home. But when we saw her mum at the school gates in their big van she smiled and waved at us like she always used to.

"Your mum does look a lot brighter." Fliss gave Lyndz's arm a little squeeze.

"Yeah, she'll be fine now!" Frankie reassured her.

Lyndz gave us a little grin and ran to the van. As we waved her off, Rosie whispered:

"I hope she will be OK. I hate seeing her so down."

I thought about Lyndz all the way home. And spookily, the first thing Mum said to me as I got through the door was:

"Have you got a minute, Laura? I want a word about Lyndz."

"Crikey Mum, how long have you been able to read minds?" I asked her. Although actually that was a pretty silly question – Mum *always* seems to know when I've done something wrong.

Mum ignored me. "Lyndz's mum came to see me today. I think things are getting a bit on top of her at the moment."

I nodded. "I know."

"Well," Mum continued, "I've had a word with your father and he agrees with me. What Patsy needs is a complete rest – away from the house, away from the chores, away from Cuddington."

Now if Dad suggested that, I knew it must be right. Dad's a doctor and he always knows what he's talking about. I'm going to be a doctor just like him when I'm older – after I've finished playing for Leicester City of course!

"Yeah, that sounds like a sensible diagnosis!" I agreed, stroking my chin in a serious doctor-type gesture.

"Well that's good," laughed Mum, "because I was thinking about asking Lyndz's family to come up to Scotland with us for the week. Uncle Bob has plenty of rooms, and according to your dad he just loves having a house full of people. What do you think? I wanted to run it by you first before I phoned Patsy."

"That's a great idea!" I ran over to Mum and gave her one of my Kenny Specials (that's when I hug someone so tightly they go red in the face and start gasping for air!).

"Phew! I'm glad you're so pleased," Mum spluttered, releasing herself from my grip.

"I think it will do them all the world of good. I'll go and phone Patsy now."

As she was dialling the number, she added, "And it means that you'll have a friend there too, seeing as Molly's taking Carli."

"She's WHAT?" I screamed. "Since when?"

"Since last night when she asked me. Is there a problem? Oh, hello there, Patsy..."

A *problem,* she says! Not much! Molly the horrible Monster is bad enough on her own, but when she's with her gruesome best mate Carli it's Nightmare City!

Still, at least if I had Lyndz with me it would be two against two. And I was sure that with all our devious Sleepover tricks we could get the better of them!

Actually, just thinking that made me a bit sad. I wished ALL the Sleepover gang could come up to Scotland with us. I mean, I really really like Lyndz and everything, but it seemed a bit mean going away with just one of my friends. I felt guilty somehow, as though I'd sort of betrayed the others.

"Pull yourself together, McKenzie!" I told myself sternly. "The others won't see it that way. They'll just be glad that Lyndz is going to have a good holiday!"

Boy was I wrong about that!

The next morning when I got to school, Lyndz was as frisky as a new puppy. She was laughing and joking and larking about.

"What's got into you?" Frankie was teasing her as I walked up to them. "Has someone put happy sugar in your Ready Brek or something?"

"Kenny! Kenny! I'm so glad you've arrived!" Lyndz rushed up to me and almost swung me off my feet. "I didn't want to say anything until you were here too."

The others looked at me questioningly.

"Isn't it great?" Lyndz gushed. "Kenny's mum rang last night to see if we'd all like to go up to Scotland with them at half-term. Isn't that brill?"

"Fantastic!"

"Excellent!"

The others all started leaping about too. They were taking the news better than I'd expected.

"Where will we stay?" Rosie wondered.

"What kind of clothes will I have to bring?" Fliss demanded.

Whoa, girls!

"Erm, no, I think you've got it wrong," I mumbled. "Mum asked Lyndz and *her family*."

"Mrs McKenzie told Mum we'd be doing her a favour because she could do with some sensible adult company," Lyndz explained quietly, suddenly aware that she'd just rammed her great size nines into her gob. "But Stuart and Tom aren't coming," she carried on, as if that made the slightest bit of difference. "Mum's sister Lorraine is going to stay at our place to keep an eye on them."

"Kenny?" Frankie stared at me. "Why didn't you tell us about this?"

"I-I-I didn't know until yesterday," I stammered. "I didn't really…"

My voice trailed off as I suddenly saw Lyndz looking very troubled.

"I'm really glad you're coming, Lyndz," I told her truthfully. "We'll have a great time. IT'LL DO YOU GOOD!" I added meaningfully, looking at the others.

The whistle went for the start of school, and I've never been as glad to hear it in my life! I felt bad about the others, but I couldn't help thinking that they were being a bit mean to poor old Lyndz.

During the morning when we had to split up into groups for project work, Fliss, Rosie and Frankie quickly huddled together, leaving Lyndz and me by ourselves. Even Mrs Weaver our teacher raised her eyes at that. And at breaktime, although they hung round with us they kept making catty remarks about how they were going to have the "best sleepover ever" during half-term.

"What a pity you two won't be there to join in!" Fliss told me and Lyndz sarcastically. "But you obviously prefer each other's company nowadays."

By lunchtime Lyndz was a dithering wreck. We were all sitting on a bench when she announced:

"Look, I'm going to tell Mum that we can't come away with you, Kenny. It's my fault that we've all fallen out and I can't bear it!"

Her chin started to tremble and her eyes filled with tears.

"Right then, are you satisfied now?" I turned on the others angrily. "Lyndz needs a holiday more than anyone. It just so happens that it's going to be with me. If there was a way to invite you all up to Scotland I would, believe me. But Great Uncle Bob's about ninety or something. I don't think it would be very good for his health if we *all* descended on him, do you?"

The others shook their heads and looked suitably ashamed. They gave Lyndz an extra big hug.

"Sorry for being so mean," Frankie told her. "You go and have fun – just not *too* much, OK?"

At least we were all friends again, which was the main thing. But my big speech back there had got me thinking. Why couldn't we all go up to Scotland? Uncle Bob wasn't *really* ninety, and Dad had already said that he had loads of rooms and loved having his house full of people. What could be better than having it full of my friends? I knew that

Mum would be speaking to him that night to confirm the arrangements, so I'd have to ask her if the rest of the gang could come with us before she phoned.

All afternoon I rehearsed how I would ask her. The only problem was that as far as Mum was concerned, us Sleepover girls together meant only one thing – TROUBLE. And it was one thing coping with that in your own home, but quite another transporting it hundreds of miles up into the wilds of Scotland.

I decided to just grab the bull by the horns and ask Mum straight out as soon as I got home. But it was just my luck that she was tackling Dad's paperwork. Now if there's one thing I've learnt in my ten years on this planet, it is *never* to disturb Mum when she's got her business-head on. The fall-out can be pretty spectacular – I still have the scars to prove it! And it was the worst luck ever that she had her business-head on all through dinner and all through the rest of the evening. In fact she only snapped out of it when the phone rang.

"Oh Uncle Bob!" she spoke crisply into the receiver. "I was just about to ring you."

Drat, drat and double blooming drat covered in bogies. I was too late – there was no way that the rest of the Sleepover gang could come up to Scotland with us now!

CHAPTER THREE

Whilst Mum chatted to Great Uncle Bob, I sat on the stairs and put my head in my hands. I'd let my chums down big time. I know that they weren't expecting to go to Scotland with us or anything, but I'd kind of got used to the idea in my head.

I'd never been to Great Uncle Bob's house before, but I imagined it was like this enormous castle overlooking a lake. I figured that it would have about fifty bedrooms and they'd all have four-poster beds and jacuzzi baths just like the one Fliss has, only much bigger. I imagined the five of us swimming in the lake. Well, maybe Fliss wouldn't actually swim in the lake, she'd just hover at the edge looking pretty…

"… Laura! Laura! For goodness sake, stop daydreaming! Uncle Bob wants a word with you!" Mum was holding out the receiver to me and looking very impatient.

What on earth could he want with me? I hadn't been listening to Mum's conversation at all, so I didn't know what she'd told him about Lyndz and her family. Maybe he was going to explain to me why they couldn't stay with us after all. I braced myself for the worst.

"Er, h-hello?" I stammered, taking the phone from Mum.

"Kenny! How are you?" a warm chuckly voice asked.

Now any adult who calls me Kenny instead of my stupid proper name is all right by me.

"Fine thanks!" I grinned.

"So I'm finally going to meet you *and* one of your friends – two for the price of one, eh?" he guffawed.

"Erm yes, thanks for letting Lyndz come

too, Great Uncle Bob," I said. "We really appreciate it."

"The more the merrier. How are the rest of your Sleepover chums?" he asked.

Well, you could have knocked me down with a feather! How on earth did he know about *them*?

"Erm, fine thanks," I whispered. I was beginning to see why Mum thought the guy was a bit strange.

"It seems such a pity that only one of your friends is going to accompany you up to Bonny Scotland. How about inviting the others as well? What are their names again? Frankie, Fliss and who's the other one?"

The guy was seriously starting to spook me out now.

"R-Rosie!" I squeaked.

"Ah yes, that's the one!" he chuckled. "I love reading about your sleepover exploits in your Christmas letters!"

Phew! So that's how he knew about the Sleepover gang. (Mum makes us write these stupid letters to our rellies at Crimbo time and I always fill mine with stuff about our best sleepovers and of course news of Leicester City FC!)

Anyway, when I'd recovered myself I suddenly realised what Great Uncle Bob had suggested. It was like he could really read my mind!

"Thanks, Great Uncle Bob!" I screamed. "That'd be brilliant! I'll ask them all tomorrow."

"Oh Kenny – there's just one thing before you go."

"Yes?"

"Do you think you could just call me 'Uncle Bob'? I don't want to feel like a doting old fool just yet!"

I grinned. "OK Uncle Bob, you've got it. See ya!"

I handed the phone over to Dad, who was hovering by my shoulder. This was just *wicked*! I couldn't wait to see the others at school the next day. But I was going to make sure that I had some fun with them first.

The next morning I was in the playground first for once. As soon as Rosie appeared, I started doing this crazy jig.

"You look like a turkey with a firework up its bottom!" she shrieked. "What on earth are you doing?"

"The highland fling!" I shouted, throwing myself into my dancing with gusto. "Lyndz and I have to learn it for Uncle Bob's party. It's going to be wicked."

"Oh!" Rosie's face fell. "Right."

"Yeah, he has this mega big party every year and we're going to be there for it. It's going to be ace! Hey Lyndz, I'm going to have to teach you the highland fling before we go up to Scotland, you know!"

Lyndz was walking into the playground with Frankie and Fliss. She looked kind of embarrassed when I mentioned the Scottish trip, like she didn't want to upset the others or something. But I didn't let that stop me.

"Uncle Bob's got this stonking great pile of a house. It's really mega. You'd love it, guys!" I looked round the others then clapped my hand over my mouth. "Oops sorry, I forgot! Still, Lyndz and I'll tell you all about it when we get back, won't we?"

Lyndz just went bright red and looked at

her feet. The others looked seriously peeved.

But I didn't stop there. By lunchtime I'd told them that Uncle Bob had hundreds of servants, including chefs who could knock up any delicacy you fancied. I'd also told them how all the guests at his party would be in the height of fashion and dripping in diamonds. You should have seen their faces! Honestly, if looks could kill, I'd be dead a million times over.

I was just about to launch into a description of Uncle Bob's (imaginary) helicopter and speedboat when Frankie snarled:

"OK McKenzie, I think we get the picture! You and Lyndz are going to have a fantastic time in Scotland and we're not. Well quite frankly I pity Lyndz. I wouldn't want to spend all my half-term with such a bragger. I don't know what's got into you, Kenny. You're not the same girl we used to know."

The others stared at me hard and shook their heads. Even Lyndz was looking at me sadly.

"We wouldn't come to Scotland with you if you paid us, would we girls?" Frankie growled.

"No way!"

"No thanks!"

I grinned. My plan had worked.

"Well that's a pity," I said innocently. "Because I *was* going to ask you all if you wanted to come with us too!"

"You're kidding!" The others started doing impressions of goldfishes with their mouths open.

"No, straight up," I admitted. "Uncle Bob invited you himself last night. I was just winding you up to pay you back for being so mean yesterday!"

"Kenny, you creep!" Frankie leapt on to my back.

"Still, if you're not going to come it doesn't matter," I shrugged, shaking her off.

"'Course we will, you dill!" Frankie grinned. "Especially if your Uncle's place is as fantastic as you say."

"Ah well, I actually made that up!" I confessed. "I've never even been there myself. It could be one big run-down old shack for all I know."

"Oh well, in that case," Rosie said jokingly,

"I don't think we should go. What do you think, Fliss?"

"Well erm, I don't think Mum would let me go anyway," Fliss admitted sheepishly.

"WHAT?" I almost screamed. "You gave Lyndz and me such a hard time yesterday because you weren't coming with us and now you say you can't come anyway? There's no pleasing some people!"

"Mum needs me to help out with the twins," Fliss told us huffily. "She's always saying how she'd be lost without me."

"But you will ask her, won't you Fliss? It'll be a laugh," Frankie giggled.

Then she turned to me. "Kenny, you are serious about this, aren't you? This isn't another one of your sick jokes?"

"I'm seriously serious," I reassured them. "Just ask your parents tonight and let me know tomorrow."

I felt all kind of warm and happy as we walked home from school. Not only would Lyndz be having a better half-term than she expected – we all would!

I thought the worst thing about the whole

deal would be waiting until the following day to see whether the others could go. But that evening our phone was ringing hot on the hook. And do you know who the first person to ring was? Only Mrs Proudlove, Fliss's mum.

As soon as I heard her voice on the other end I thought, "Oh-oh, trouble." We'd never hear the end of it if Fliss really couldn't go, because as you well know she hates being left out of anything. And her mum does tend to fuss over nothing. I just knew that she would be panicking about how far away Scotland was, and who would be taking care of her precious baby in her absence.

Well, it just goes to show how much *I* know.

"That was Fliss's mum," said Mum as she came off the phone about three hours later. Hell-o Mum, I knew that, I answered the phone, remember?

"She just rang to check arrangements for Scotland and to thank us for taking Fliss with us."

"What?" I asked, stunned. "You mean she can come?"

"She certainly can! Nikki seemed quite relieved to have her off her hands, to be honest with you."

Now that I could believe.

Ten seconds later the phone rang again. It was Frankie.

"I can come, I can come!" she squealed down the phone. "Is your mum around so my mum can discuss the arrangements with her?"

Whilst Mum was still on the phone Molly returned from Carli's.

"Who's that?" She gestured to the phone.

"Frankie's mum. Not that it's any of your business!"

"What did *she* want, then?" Molly demanded as soon as Mum had put the phone down. But I could guess by her aggressive tone that she'd already figured out the answer.

"Uncle Bob asked me to invite the rest of my mates to Scotland with us," I smiled evilly. "I guess he knows that you've only got the one friend to invite!"

Molly made a lunge for me.

"That'll do, you two," said Mum sharply. "If there's going to be any trouble, neither of you will be coming. You can go and stay at Gran's with Emma."

I should explain that Emma our older sister had to study for exams over half-term, so she was staying with our grandparents in Cuddington.

"Well, how are we all going to get up there?" Molly demanded. "There won't be enough room in our car."

Oh no! I hadn't even thought about that! Fortunately Mum had.

"I know that, Molly. That's why Lyndz's parents will be taking all the girls in their van."

Wicked!

The only person we hadn't heard from was Rosie-Posie, and I just knew that there wouldn't be a problem with her. Her mum's always a bit strapped for cash since her dad left, and they never get much of a chance to get away. I knew that she'd be keen to let Rosie have a break with us.

Well, I was wrong again! When I got to school the next morning, the others were all in a huddle in the playground. I figured they'd all be chatting excitedly about Scotland, but they looked dead miserable.

"Whassup?" I rushed over to them.

"Rosie can't come with us," Fliss said quietly.

"No! Why not?"

"It's Mum's new boyfriend Richard, he wants us all to go somewhere together," Rosie sniffed. "I tried to persuade Mum, really I did, but there was no way she was going to budge. She really likes this guy and she said this was really important to her. What could I do?"

Rosie put her hands over her eyes and her shoulders started to shake. Fliss put her arm round her and Lyndz and Frankie looked glumly at their feet.

I felt gutted. It just wouldn't be the same if we weren't all together.

"I don't know what to say Rosie, I really don't," I admitted. "We're just not going to enjoy Scotland so much now, are we guys?"

Nobody said anything. I looked at Frankie – and I swear she was *laughing*! Lyndz was bright red in the face and starting to splutter, and Fliss was trying so hard not to laugh that she was snorting down her nose.

"Guys?"

"FOOLED YOU!" they all yelled together.

"You're not the only one who can wind people up, you know!" giggled Rosie, slapping me on the shoulder.

"You mean you *can* come?" I asked, gobsmacked.

"'Course I can!" Rosie smiled. "Richard had mentioned about going away but when I told him about your Great Uncle Bob's place he said it sounded a lot of fun and I should definitely go. He says we can go away another time. Isn't that cool?"

"Not as cool as us all going away together!" I said, and we all started doing a crazy jig right there in the middle of the playground.

"Well, Uncle Bob, you'd better watch out!" I sang. "'Cos Scotland here we come!"

CHAPTER FOUR

For the next few days, right up until half-term, all we could talk about was Scotland and what a wicked time we were going to have. I swear that even our breath turned tartan.

Fliss's main concern was – surprise, surprise – what clothes she was going to take.

"I've got this cool little mini kilt with a dinky pin, and an Aran sweater – that's Scottish, isn't it? And I saw these great checked cropped trousers in Gap, Mum might buy those for me too."

"Get a life!" I scoffed. "All Mum said was that you should take plenty of warm things and some sturdy walking shoes. So that doesn't mean your silver stilettos, all right Fliss?"

"But what about the party?" asked Rosie. "Surely we'll need something posh for that."

"I doubt it. The villagers who go won't exactly expect to see us wearing tiaras," I reassured her. "Just take whatever's comfortable. I know what I'll be wearing…"

"… Your Leicester City football kit!" chimed in the others. "Yes, we know!"

"Although I do think you ought to make a bit of an effort for your Great Uncle," Fliss told me seriously. "You don't want to let him down, do you?"

How I stopped myself from punching her in the hooter I'll never know. Fliss gets me like that sometimes. And the thing is, she has absolutely no idea at all that she's winding me up. Although she wound *everybody* up on the day we actually set off for Scotland – and everybody made sure she knew about that!

To be fair, it wasn't all Fliss's fault that the start of our holiday was a disaster. My dad had a hand in it too – or at least one of his patients did. Now I know that doctors are there to serve their patients. And I know that saving lives is one of the most important jobs in the whole world. But why did Mrs Fogarty decide that 10.30 on Saturday morning was the ideal time to ring Dad to say that her son was seriously ill? I mean, we were all packed up and ready to go to Lyndz's to meet up with the others.

"Mrs Fogarty, you really ought to call the surgery," Dad told her gently as we all stood around tutting and pointing at our watches. "Of course they'll see a patient if it's an emergency. No Mrs Fogarty, I wouldn't want a death on my conscience, but I am pretty... all right then Mrs Fogarty, I will come round as soon as I can."

"DAD!" Molly and I yelled together.

"Look, her son just might have meningitis and you can't play around with that. I'll be back as soon as I can. You'd better ring Patsy and Keith and explain the situation to them."

And with that, Dad grabbed his doctor's bag and flew out of the door.

Now if I was a doctor, I don't really know what I would have done. But just at that moment I wasn't thinking about being a doctor. I was just thinking about meeting up with my mates and getting up to Scotland to have some fun.

Eleven o'clock passed. And half past. It was almost midday when Dad finally reappeared. I was certain that the boy had had to go to hospital for sure.

"Well?" we asked when Dad finally came through the door. We could tell by the look on his face that it wasn't good news.

"A temperature and a runny nose. The lad has a wee cold," he told us grimly. "I spent half an hour trying to reassure the woman that her son was not on death's door, and then I had to go to the surgery to inform the other doctors. You couldn't make me a cup of tea, could you Molly love? I feel exhausted and I've still got that long drive ahead of me."

Talk about spitting feathers! We'd never get up to Scotland at this rate.

When we did eventually set off, I hadn't been in the car five minutes before I'd had a fight with Molly, called Carli a brainless chicken and been told by Mum that if I carried on I wouldn't be going to Scotland at all. Needless to say, by the time we drew up in front of Lyndz's I was well cheesed off. Not in the best of moods then to cope with Fliss bawling her eyes out and having what looked like a full-on paddy.

"What's with her?" I asked Frankie, who was looking a bit pink round the edges.

"She's just discovered that she's brought her brother Callum's bag instead of her own."

She gestured to the pyjamas covered in Pokémon and Pikachu which were scrunched up on the gravel.

"You ought to have seen her when she found out!" Rosie whispered. "She went ballistic. She flung everything out over the ground and started stamping on them."

"I bet Callum did the same when he found Fliss's frilly knicks in his bag!" I grinned. "Where is he anyway?"

"That's just the point," whispered Frankie. "He's gone to stay with their gran for a few days. But when Lyndz's mum rang Fliss's mum to find out where they were, Fliss's mum didn't know and thought they'd gone off somewhere – with Fliss's bag!"

"Trust Fliss!" I snarled. "It can't be that hard to check that you've got the right bag can it? Even for Fliss."

Was this holiday turning into a disaster or what?

"So what are we doing now?" I demanded. "Waiting for Callum to turn up?"

"No, Fliss's mum is packing her another bag and Andy's going to bring it over," Lyndz explained. "He shouldn't be long because Mum rang him ages ago. I'm really cross with Fliss, actually. Before this happened Mum was quite bright, but she's gone all cross and narky again."

"She's not the only one," I said through gritted teeth.

After what felt like an hour (but was apparently only five minutes) Andy's van appeared. He leapt out brandishing a luggage bag identical to the one whose contents were now being tried on gleefully by Ben and Spike, Lyndz's two youngest brothers.

"Here you are love," he smiled, thrusting it towards Fliss. "We managed to trace your gran and get your bag back. Now, now, there's no need to cry!"

Fliss was in full waterworks mode again and was sobbing into Andy's jumper. Mum managed to prise her away, and before any more mishaps could occur bundled us all into Lyndz's van.

"OK Jim, I've got the directions and your mobile number. You've got mine, haven't you?" Lyndz's dad checked with mine. "Right then, all being well we'll rendez-vous at Tebay service station. All aboard? Wagons roll!"

At last! We were off! I have to admit that at one stage I seriously doubted that we would ever get out of Cuddington.

"Can we have the Steps tape on, Mum?" Lyndz asked.

"Yeah!"

"Wheels On The Bus!" yelled Ben.

"Steps!" we all chorused back.

"Wheels On The Bus!" Ben's chin was going all wobbly.

"OK, you can have your tape on first, Ben," Lyndz caved in. "But then it's our turn, all right?"

Ben grinned his big soppy grin and started doing all the actions to the songs on his tapes. The first time round we all joined in and it was a bit of a laugh. But when Ben insisted on having his tape on again, my heart sank. Not least because the alternative to his stupid tape was him shrieking at the top of his voice.

"Just once more then." Lyndz shrugged her shoulders apologetically at the rest of us.

I wouldn't have cared, but Mrs Collins just didn't say anything at all. So we had to listen to "Wheels On The Stupid Bus" yet again. And let me tell you, by the fifth time I was ready to yank the wheels *off* the nearest bus and stuff them down Ben's throat.

Fortunately, five repeats of his tape seemed more than enough for Ben too, because he nodded off.

"Great!" whispered Rosie. "Can we have Steps on now?"

We handed the tape to Mrs Collins who put it on. Then, noticing that Ben was asleep, she turned the volume right down so we could barely hear it at all.

"Could we have it up just a tiny bit, Mrs Collins?" Fliss asked.

"I don't want to wake up Ben, Felicity," Lyndz's mum replied coldly. "He wouldn't be so tired if we'd managed to get off on time in the first place."

"Patsy!" Mr Collins looked crossly at his wife.

Fliss went bright red and her eyes welled up with tears. Lyndz squeezed her arm and mouthed "sorry". She looked as though she was about to start crying herself. The rest of us just looked miserable. So much for Mum's plan of bringing Lyndz's mum away with us to cheer her up. At the moment she just seemed to be making everybody else unhappy too.

At least when we got to Scotland we'd be able to escape from her for a bit. Whereas right now we were stuck in the van with hardly any music, one snoring toddler and a baby who, by the smell of it, had just filled his nappy.

It was a major relief when we finally pulled into the service station next to Dad's car. But it made us feel worse then ever when we entered the café and found Molly and Carli in sickeningly high spirits.

"We've had a wicked journey!" Molly gushed. "We've listened to two Westlife tapes and Robbie Williams. We even caught Dad singing along to them."

"Yeah, it was so funny I thought I was going to wet myself!"

"Carli!" Mum pretended to sound shocked. "What kind of journey have you lot had then? Noisy, I'll bet!"

"Erm, not exactly," I said truthfully, but I couldn't expand on that because Lyndz's mum had appeared looking tired and harassed.

"I didn't realise it was such a long way," she sighed, flopping down on the seat next to Mum's.

"Not to worry Patsy, the bulk of it's behind us now," Mum reassured her. "There's only a couple of hours to go."

"Two hours!" Frankie almost exploded. "I'm not sure I can stand that van for another two hours."

She said that last bit quietly because she didn't want Lyndz's mum to hear. It was true that the thought of two more hours cooped up with Mrs Trunchbull's more gruesome sister didn't seem a very exciting prospect. But it also meant that in two hours we'd be at Uncle Bob's place with a week of adventures in front of us!

In actual fact, the last two hours of the journey passed really quickly. It was very dark by the time we set off again, and we were soon in the countryside where there didn't seem to be too many streetlights. The darkness and the rhythm of the moving van seemed to make us all drowsy and I can't really remember anything much until Mr Collins suddenly shouted:

"Wake up guys! We're almost there!"

It was amazing, because one minute I was fast asleep and the next I was wide awake, staring eagerly out of the window.

For ages we couldn't really see anything.

We seemed to be driving up a long, long road with trees on one side and a huge expanse of water on the other.

"Look, a lake!" I pointed to it eagerly. "I knew there'd be a lake!"

Occasionally we caught sight of a startled pair of eyes on the road in front of us – rabbits, foxes, goodness knows what else.

"This is amazing!" breathed Mrs Collins softly.

Suddenly Mr Collins slowed down.

"Oh my goodness!" he gasped. "I didn't expect this!"

We all peered eagerly out of the windows. Looming before us beneath a sinister swirling mist was the creepiest, spookiest house I had ever seen in my life.

CHAPTER FIVE

"Th-this is a joke, right?" spluttered Fliss, stumbling from the van. "We're n-not really going to stay here, are we?"

I was kind of wondering whether it was one of Dad's jokes myself when the door of the house creaked open.

"A monster!" screeched Fliss and Rosie together, ducking down behind the van.

It was the funniest monster I'd ever seen. There in the doorway, silhouetted by the lights from the hall behind him, was a tiny little bloke dressed in a kilt and funny long socks. He was warbling *Scotland the Brave* and doing a strange little dance.

I saw Mum raise her eyes at Lyndz's mum. But miracle of miracles, Lyndz's mum was actually doubled over with laughter.

"Hello there, Bob!" Dad called out and climbed the steps to join him. "You've dressed the part for our Sassenach friends, I see!"

"Indeed laddie," Uncle Bob was shaking Dad's hand with gusto. "Can't be doing with the bairns thinking we Scots are a dour lot!"

"What's he talking about?" hissed Frankie in my ear. "I haven't understood one word. I didn't realise Scottish people spoke a different language!"

"Me neither," I agreed.

"Come in, come in," Uncle Bob gestured towards the rest of us. "You must be weary fit to drop. Mrs Barber's preparing the best hot chocolate north of the border, so come in and rest your bones a wee while afore bed."

"Come on girls, let's get you all inside." Lyndz's mum rounded us up with Ben asleep in one arm and Spike nodding off in the other. "This is going to be a fun week, I can just tell!"

We all exchanged glances. She was like a completely different person, all bubbly and bright like she used to be.

"It must be something in the air," I muttered.

"I'd better bottle some and take it home with us!" Lyndz giggled.

"I want to go home!" Fliss sobbed. "This place is just too – *weird*!"

"Come on Fliss, we're just tired, that's all," Frankie reassured her. "Things will look different in the morning – I promise!"

"I-if we're still here by then," Fliss stammered. "We'll probably have been b-bitten by a v-vampire or something!" And she burst into tears again.

"Now don't you worry about that, Fliss," I comforted her as I helped to carry her bag inside. "Frankie and I are expert vampire slayers, aren't we Franks? No big-toothed bloodsucker would *dare* mess with you, OK?"

I executed a few high kicks along with a bloodcurdling scream to prove my point.

Unfortunately the entrance hall was so vast that my scream sort of magnified and bounced off the walls. It sounded as though a mass-murderer was on the rampage in one of the rooms upstairs.

Frankie rolled her eyes at me as Fliss went off on another of her sob-fests.

"Now Kenny, you'll arouse the ghosties with noises like that!" Uncle Bob appeared in the hall in front of us. "This way for hot chocolate, then I'll show you all to your rooms."

We followed him in silence, trying to take in the vastness of the house. I know that I'd sort of dreamt that Uncle Bob lived in a castle, but I never thought it would be anything as enormous as this. The ceilings were so high that you had to strain your neck to look up at them. The walls were all wood-panelled with various deer heads mounted on plaques above us.

"Ooh, gross!" Frankie (the vegetarian) shuddered theatrically. "Killing animals like that is just disgusting!"

Fortunately Uncle Bob didn't seem to have heard. He led us into a room where an enormous fire roared in a massive stone fireplace. On a huge wooden table were steaming cups of the most gorgeous hot chocolate you have ever tasted in your life. Mmm, I can still taste it now – scrum-my!

"It looks to me like you all need your beds," Uncle Bob grinned as we were starting to doze by the fire. "Bairns first, follow me."

We all stared at him.

"He means you lot!" Dad laughed, pointing to Molly, Carli, my mates and me. "Off you go then, sleep well!"

Uncle Bob bounded up the stairs as we followed as quickly as we could, lugging our bags up with us.

"Here we have Molly and Carli's room." He flung open a door to reveal a pretty room with two enormous beds covered in rose-patterned eiderdowns. The curtains were all swagged and lamps cast a rosy glow.

"Cool!" Molly gasped.

Fliss looked in jealously. "It looks nice in there," she agreed. "I wouldn't mind sleeping in there myself!"

"With Molly?" Lyndz groaned. "You must be mad."

"Now I thought you lassies would all like to be together for your sleepover shenanigans," Uncle Bob told us as we walked a little further down the landing. "So I've put you all in here."

He flung open the door to reveal an absolutely ginormous room. It looked about as big as one of our classrooms. There were five beds all covered in sprigged bedspreads with a mountain of blankets underneath.

"I'll need a leg up to get in there!" Rosie giggled.

"The bathroom's just across the way," Uncle Bob pointed. "And don't you go minding the strange noises. Things tend to go bump in the night but it's usually only the hot water pipes. Nightie-night, sleep well."

He closed the door and left.

"I'm n-not sure about this." Fliss leant against her bed. "It's s-so s-spooky!"

"No it's not Fliss, it's exciting. Look at that!" I went to the far end of the room and pulled back the curtains. The night outside was thick and dark.

"Look at the moon! It's just—"

But I couldn't go on, because something had just flown past the window. It was something small and black, I was sure it was. I blinked hard. Maybe I was more tired than I thought and was imagining things. No, there was another one. Something with big wings. A shiver crept down my spine.

"What's up, Kenz?" Frankie demanded, coming to join me.

"I-I've just seen something fly past the window," I told her. "But I don't know what it was."

Fliss started howling and Rosie and Lyndz ran to comfort her.

"That's enough, Kenny," Frankie said sternly, snatching the curtains and drawing them together roughly. "You never know when to stop, do you? Fliss is already freaked out and you pull a stunt like that. Enough, OK?"

"But…" I protested, but I could tell by the look on Frankie's face that there was no point continuing.

"I'm sorry Fliss, I guess we're all a bit tired." I leapt up on to her bed. "I didn't mean to scare you – honest!"

Fliss sniffed and smiled weakly.

"Let's push the beds closer together so it feels more cosy," Lyndz suggested.

"Good idea, Batman," I agreed, and we heaved and shoved until they were all together at the end of the room nearest the door.

"Come on, let's get the bathroom stuff over with," Rosie suggested. "I don't know about you but I feel I could sleep for a week!"

"Well don't do that, Rosie-Posie," I punched her lightly on the arm. "'Cos we've got a week of Scottish fun ahead of us, remember!"

Now we might have had a week of excitement ahead of us, but that night was no picnic, I can tell you. Fliss was moaning and shivering on one side of me, and Lyndz was snoring her head off opposite. Fun it was not. We didn't even have a midnight feast because we were so tired. I was glad when it was morning so we could start to explore.

Over a mammoth breakfast of porridge and toast Uncle Bob told us, "Just you lassies make yourselves at home. It's good to have some young blood in the house again."

"Do you reckon *he's* a vampire then?" I whispered to Frankie.

She just mouthed, "You idiot!" and whacked my leg under the table.

"Just steer clear of the loch, it is very deep," Uncle Bob continued. "And it might be sensible to come inside when it starts dropping dark – you can see all sorts of shapes lurking among the trees at dusk. I wouldn'ae want you to be scared now!"

Fliss gasped and looked very anxious again.

"He is joking Fliss," Mum said firmly, frowning as Uncle Bob left the room. "But I don't want you roaming about in the dark anyway, it can get very cold. Just go and amuse yourselves quietly and we'll see you back here for lunch at one."

We all ran off, whooping and hollering. The first room we discovered was a library lined with books from floor to ceiling.

"Wow!" breathed Frankie. "I didn't think one person could own so many books!"

Then we practised skidding down the hallway in our socks for ages, until Ben found us and wanted to join in.

"'Snot fair!" he whimpered as Lyndz's mum scooped him up and carried him away.

"Sorry girls!" she called over her shoulder.

"Your mum certainly seems a lot happier!" Rosie said.

"I know!" Lyndz grinned. "She said she'd had the best night's sleep she's had in months. And she's really excited about helping to get everything ready for the party too. It's great!"

It certainly was great to see Lyndz looking so much happier too.

Running upstairs we could hear music thumping out of Molly and Carli's room.

"We come all this way and they stay in their room listening to tapes!" I tutted. "They could do that anywhere. How could they pass up the chance to explore this great house?"

"Where do you suppose this leads?" asked Fliss, turning a door handle. "It's not one of the bedrooms."

She opened the door a crack and we peered into the darkness.

"There are some stairs," said Rosie excitedly. "It must lead to the attic!"

We all looked at each other and shrieked, "Jeanne!" Then we burst out laughing.

We must have told you about the time we stayed in a hotel in Paris and nearly scared ourselves stupid because we thought someone was being held prisoner in the attic?

"I hope exploring up here's not going to be as terrifying as last time!" Fliss shivered. "At least there's no creepy maid this time. Boy, was that Chantal scary!"

"Wasn't she just!" Rosie laughed.

We'd reached the top of the stairs and the attic looked pretty empty.

"No prisoners here!" Frankie announced.

"Only that blimming noise from Molly's stupid tapes!" I snarled.

"If we follow the noise we can work out where her room is!" Frankie suggested.

"Excellent!"

The attic itself was vast with not much in

it at all, just a few piles of dusty papers and some empty packing cases. We crept silently along, occasionally stopping to listen to the noises below us.

"Listen, I can hear Mum talking to Spike," Lyndz whispered. "We must be above the boys' room."

"And we're definitely getting nearer to Molly's room," Fliss whispered. "The noise is getting louder."

We crept on a little further until we were standing directly over the music. The floor felt as though it was moving slightly from the vibrations.

"I'm surprised she's not deaf listening to it that loud!" Rosie murmured.

"If we leap up and down she'll probably think it's part of the song!" Lyndz laughed.

"Well she would if we did it now!" I grinned. "But it wouldn't half give her a shock if we did it in the middle of the night!"

"You wouldn't!" Fliss looked part shocked, part scared.

"Well let's just say – it depends," I told them thoughtfully. "But, just in case, we'd better mark out exactly where Molly's room is."

We dragged a couple of packing cases over to roughly mark out the boundaries.

"Now if that sister of mine pulls just *one* stunt this week," I told the others firmly, "we're going to let her have it – big time!"

CHAPTER SIX

All the time we were having lunch we kept eyeballing Molly and Carli and laughing.

"Grow up!" Molly yelled at last. "You're just so immature! Ignore them, Carli."

"Molly for goodness sake, we've come away on holiday! Can't you and Laura forget your differences for once?" Mum snapped.

"Not likely!"

"Well there's plenty of room for you to stay out of each other's way then," Mum replied tartly. "And it might not do you and Carli any harm to get some fresh air. You can listen to your tapes any time. The air is so clean here, you ought to make the most of it before we go home."

Molly rolled her eyes and made a being-sick face behind Mum's back. Then she turned to me.

"You're dead!" she muttered before stomping out, with Carli in close pursuit.

"I'm so scared!" I pretended to quake in my shoes.

"What have you girls got planned for this afternoon?" asked Lyndz's mum.

"Exploring outside!"

"Well don't stay out too late," Mum warned us. "It gets dark a bit earlier up here. And for goodness sake, stay out of trouble!"

"Mother!" I looked at her innocently. "We *always* stay out of trouble!"

"If only I could believe that!" Mum sighed.

We grabbed our coats and, whooping and yelling, ran like mad things to the edge of the lake (or "loch" as Uncle Bob called it).

"It's amazing!" Fliss breathed. "It looks like something out of a fairytale!"

"That it is, Felicity!" Uncle Bob had appeared silently behind us. "If ever I have any troubles, I bring myself here and they all seem to sort themselves out."

"I could sort out all my troubles by pushing Molly into the loch," I grumbled. "And holding her under!"

Uncle Bob laughed. He picked a few stones from the ground, then one by one he skimmed them across the lake so that they bounced along the surface, once, twice, even three times.

"That's wicked!" Rosie gasped. "Could you teach us how to do that?"

"I reckon so!" he smiled. "First you've got to find nice flat stones – not too small and not too big."

We hunted at our feet.

"Now then, stand at an angle to the loch and focus. The action's all in the wrist. Relax, then whip it, like this."

His stone skimmed the lake in four easy bounces.

"Now you try!"

Our stones just plopped in.

"Try again!"

Uncle Bob encouraged us and helped us

with our aim. Just when we were starting to get a bit bored, Fliss's stone skipped twice along the lake's surface.

"I did it, I did it!" She leapt up and down.

That spurred us on to try harder and eventually we all managed it. It felt fantastic, a real sense of achievement!

"It's a wee bit nippy!" Uncle Bob shivered. "But I know what'll warm you up!"

He led us away from the lake to a clearing where Dad and Mr Collins were sawing logs.

"I've got us some helpers!" he grinned.

Dad looked apprehensive. "I'm not sure about that Bob, saws can be pretty dangerous."

"Och, not when I'm supervising. Calm yourself, Jim," Uncle Bob replied.

First Frankie and I had a go at sawing, then Lyndz and Fliss. Finally Rosie had a go with Uncle Bob. When we weren't sawing we were helping to stack up the logs in great piles. I'd never got so hot, nor ached so much in my life, not even playing football.

"Right lassies, it's almost dusk now!" Uncle Bob told us at last. "Time for a wee romp outside afore it's time to go in. I'd check out the chapel by the loch if I were you. I've heard tell of great goings-on down there at about this time. You must have a look – if you're brave enough, that is!"

"W-what does he mean?" Fliss looked at us anxiously as we walked away towards the lake again.

"Ah, nothing, Fliss! You should know by now that Uncle Bob's just a big wind-up merchant. He just wants to tease us, that's all," I reassured her.

But as we approached the lake I wasn't so sure. The light seemed to have faded in just a short time and everything seemed to be casting freaky shadows around us. The wind was whistling through the trees, twisting the branches into sinister shapes.

"I don't like this!" Fliss hung back. "Let's go back to the house – please!"

"We'll just have a quick look at the chapel first," I promised.

A dark shell of a building stood between the lake and the house, its roof caving in and its walls starting to crumble.

"Oooh, well spooky!" Frankie shuddered.

We stopped a little way from it, too scared to go any nearer.

"D-did you see that?" Lyndz gasped suddenly. "I'm sure I just saw a shadow moving about in there!"

"And a flash of light," I mumbled.

"I can hear strange noises," Rosie shuddered. "Let's get out of here!"

I was starting to feel knotted up and sick inside. This really was a bit too scary. Fliss was shaking and crying.

"I want to go home," she sobbed. "This is frightening me now."

I tried to pull myself together.

"Now what would Buffy do in a situation like this?" I asked. "She wouldn't wimp out, would she?"

I took a deep breath and did a few high kicks and karate moves with my arms. I tried to yell something fierce but my voice came out in a reedy wail.

Suddenly a twig cracked behind me and I sensed someone watching me from the shadows. Instinctively I lashed back with my left leg and swung round with my right arm.

"Watch it, you moron!"

"MOLLY!" we all yelled together.

She stepped into the clearing, clutching her side where my foot had caught her. She flashed a torch on the others.

"Mum told me I had to come out here and find you," she snarled. "I wish I hadn't bothered!"

"It was you!" Rosie and Frankie gasped in relief.

"Thought you'd scare us, did you?" I snarled back, the strength flooding back into my voice. "Well, you'll have to do better than that!"

"What are they on about, Molly?" Carli looked puzzled.

"Don't come the innocent!" I snapped. "We're on to you two!"

Molly tapped her head with her finger and pulled a face at Carli.

"Mental!" she mouthed.

Boy was I mad! I swear that I'd have strangled her there and then if Mum hadn't appeared to round us up for supper.

Mrs Barber, with a little help from Mum and Mrs Collins, had prepared this amazing meal. We started with thick soup. Then she brought out these enormous *wild-boar* sausages and huge bowls of mashed potato. It was the best I'd ever tasted, I could live on it forever! The sausages were kind of strong-tasting but good. Fliss and Rosie weren't too keen, but fortunately Mrs Barber had prepared a vegetable casserole for Frankie because she doesn't eat meat, so they shared that. For pudding it was treacle tart and custard – *fan-tastic*!

We all helped Mrs Barber to clear away, then we went to flop in the lounge where we'd had hot chocolate the night before. Uncle Bob lit loads of candles and the adults sat on the big squashy sofas whilst the rest of us lay around on the floor by the fire. It was wicked, especially when Uncle Bob started telling us all these spooky stories.

"Some say you can hear a wailing in a chapel not too far from here," he told us in a voice so low that you had to strain your ears to hear him. "It belongs to Flora McDonald.

The poor wee lassie turned up on her wedding day to discover that her fiancé had been killed in a hunting accident. She went mad with grief and killed herself right there in front of the altar. If you listen hard you can hear the swish of her wedding dress as her ghost wanders through the chapel. Some have even seen a figure dressed in white wandering through the grounds."

"AHH!" Fliss screamed. "Not here? Not the chapel we went to today?"

"No, not that chapel, Fliss," Mum said very firmly. "Not *any* chapel, right Uncle Bob? These are just folktales, aren't they? And ones that aren't very suitable just before bedtime if I might say so!"

"Aye, you're right, Valerie," Uncle Bob grinned. "Don't mind an old fool with more tales to tell than sense. Now Felicity, I didn'ae mean to upset you. How about hot chocolate all round, Mrs Barber?"

"I think we'll take ours to our room with us if that's OK," I said when Mrs Barber appeared back with a tray full of steaming mugs. The others looked at me, amazed.

"We're very tired, aren't we?" I stared at them hard.

"Oh yes, 'course, all that sawing you know!" Frankie followed my lead. "Night everybody!"

The others followed us out of the sitting room and we all trooped upstairs to our bedroom.

"Couldn't we have stayed downstairs a bit longer?" Fliss asked apprehensively. "You know, with the others."

"No Fliss, we've got business to attend to," I told her, leaping on to my bed. "Molly and Carli business. They scared us outside, remember, so now it's payback time!"

I pointed to the attic. The others squashed on to my bed and, huddling together, we formed our grand plan. When it was all sorted we did high fives and ran giggling into the bathroom. It was important that we were ready to go as soon as we figured that Molly and Carli were settled down for the night.

It seemed like about five hours before they even came up to bed, and another hour before they'd finished in the bathroom.

"What are they *doing* in there?" Frankie sounded exasperated.

"Molly's so ugly she needs about a million potions to hold her face together," I snorted. "One day it'll probably crack up completely and fall off!"

By the time they'd emerged from the bathroom Lyndz had dozed off so we had to wake her up.

"Wassup!" she grumbled.

"Come on, sleepy-head. It's action time!"

We crept to the door. I was just about to reach for the handle when I could hear footsteps along the passageway.

"It sounds like everybody else is coming to bed now!" I grumbled.

We crept back into bed and had to wait again until we were sure that the coast was clear.

"Everybody ready?" I whispered as we huddled for a second time behind the door. "Everybody know what we're supposed to be doing?"

With excited butterflies chasing about in my tummy I reached for the door handle.

Instead of the door creaking open, as I'd expected, the handle shot off in my hand! There was a *clunk* on the landing as the knob on the other side fell off too.

"What's happened?" asked Fliss anxiously.

"Erm, it's not looking good actually," I admitted, brandishing the knob. "We're stuck in here, and I can't see how we're going to get out."

CHAPTER SEVEN

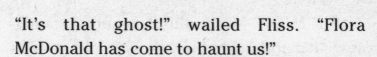

"It's that ghost!" wailed Fliss. "Flora McDonald has come to haunt us!"

"Don't be so stupid!" I snapped. "There's got to be some perfectly sensible explanation…"

Frankie was crouched by the door, squinting through the keyhole.

"You know that perfectly sensible explanation?" she said at last, straightening herself up. "I think it's called Molly and Carli! They're on the other side of the door looking like the cats who got the cream!"

"They'll look like cats who've got the SCREAM when I get hold of them!" I fumed.

"But first we need to get out of here."

I pushed the door again, but there was no way it was going to budge.

"HELP!" Rosie and Fliss started banging on the door. "Get us out of here!"

"Love to help you!" Molly said from the other side of the door. "We can't open it from this side either. I wonder how that could have happened?"

"Yes, I wonder, young lady!" There was no mistaking Mum's voice and she sounded A-N-G-R-Y!

"But Mum!" Molly didn't sound so smug now. "It's nothing to do with us!"

"Molly, it's too late for silly games. I want that door open and I want you to get back to bed!"

"I really think it's a job for a locksmith," Lyndz's dad announced seriously.

"They'll never get one so late!" Frankie hissed. "We're going to be stuck in here all night!"

"I knew this place was doomed!" Fliss sobbed. "There's something really creepy about it."

"Now I think that's just your imagination, Felicity!"

We all spun round to see Uncle Bob grinning at us from the far corner of the room. He had suddenly appeared. Out of thin air. The door hadn't opened and the window was closed so there was no way he could have got in there…

We all took one look at him and started screaming. We clung together shrieking our heads off like we were in some really bad horror movie. And all the time Uncle Bob was watching us with this silly grin on his face. At last he chuckled:

"Girls, girls, please! There's no need to be alarmed."

"B-but how did you get in?" I squeaked nervously as soon as I'd recovered my voice. The guy was freaking me out big time.

"There's a secret doorway here, look!"

He pressed against one of the panels on the wall and it sprung open, revealing a door.

"That's amazing! Like something out of a film!" Frankie said open-mouthed, hurrying to see where it led.

"It goes into the bedroom next door," Uncle Bob explained. "That's why I gave you this room. I thought maybe your Sleepover Club might discover it for yourselves."

Suddenly Uncle Bob wasn't spooky any more. He just seemed like a little guy with a wicked sense of fun.

"*You* didn't take the doorknob off so we'd find out about this, did you?" I asked him.

"No Kenny, I wouldn'ae go to all that trouble, believe me!" he grinned. "I suggest you leave this door open tonight, just in case the doorknob gremlin decides to have another go. Although I doubt she'd dare, the mood your mother's in!"

We all laughed. Outside our room we could still hear Mum tearing a strip off Molly.

"Have a good rest now. Goodnight!" He left as quietly as he'd arrived.

Even though it was very late by the time Mum and Lyndz's mum had been in to check that we were all right, we were still wide awake.

"I guess we'll just have to have a midnight feast!" I shrugged, pretending it was just about the last thing on earth that we wanted to do.

We grabbed mini-Snickers, fizzy lollies, a carton of Pringles and mini cans of marshmallow soda from our bags and piled on to Frankie's bed.

"I thought I'd die when your Uncle Bob appeared!" giggled Rosie. "My heart stopped beating, I swear!"

"He's a pretty cool guy, isn't he?" I grinned.

"I still think he's weird!" Fliss moaned.

We all bombarded her with crisps and sweets.

"Gitoutofit!" She threw them back at us. "I mean, you have to admit it's pretty strange how he keeps appearing behind us without us even hearing him."

"He's just light on his feet," I told her. "And remember, that's exactly what *we* have to be when we get our revenge on Molly in the attic."

I was so pumped up that I would happily have gone into the attic there and then, but Frankie persuaded me that it would be more sensible to wait.

"Your mum's pretty wound up at the moment, Kenz," she reasoned. "And if she caught us pulling a stunt like that tonight she'd go into meltdown!"

I reckoned the next day was bound to drag as we waited to put our plan into action. WRONG! It actually flashed past, because we made the most *amazing* discovery when we retraced our steps from the previous evening.

"We're not going back to the chapel, are we?" Fliss looked alarmed. "You don't really think Flora McDonald's ghost will be there, do you?"

"Don't be daft Fliss, there're no such things as ghosts," I reassured her. "What *I'm* interested in are the vampires."

"WHAT?" Fliss looked like she was about to faint.

I ploughed on. "Look, we heard noises right, round an old chapel? And where does Buffy do her vampire-slaying? In a graveyard, right? Well, I reckon there might well be graves round that old chapel and I think it would be an ideal hanging-out spot for those

Scottish vamps. Especially now they've heard that there are two slayers on the scene."

I did a ferocious side-kick to prove my point. "Eh Frankie, what do you say? Do you reckon they want to try their luck with us? Maybe this is Sunnydale Mark Two!"

"You're mad!" Lyndz and Rosie were shaking their heads. "You don't really believe all that stuff, do you?"

"Sure thing!" I nodded. "Come on, I bet we can find some signs of vampire activity last night."

We got to the edge of the woods, then crept cautiously towards the chapel. It wasn't as scary as it had been the night before, but there was still something a bit eerie about the place.

"Right everyone, look out for signs," I hissed.

As we approached the chapel we all stooped close to the ground.

"What exactly are we looking for?" asked Fliss weakly.

"Footprints. Like this one!" I pointed excitedly to the ground.

There in the earth were footprints, enormous ones.

"Those weren't made by Molly and Carli, were they?" Rosie looked scared.

"There are more," Frankie pointed, "and they're all leading to the chapel."

We followed them right to the entrance of the building.

"Hey, what's this?" Lyndz bent down and picked up something from among the weeds on the ground.

"It's a c-cross!" she squealed, opening her palm so we could all see it.

A gold-coloured cross, streaked with mud, glinted faintly in the sunshine.

"You know what this means," I told the others firmly. "Someone must have been trying to protect themselves against the vampires by holding this up – then they got scared and ran away."

Fliss and Rosie made some weedy gulping noises. I moved further into the chapel to take a closer look. Frankie and Lyndz came with me, whilst Fliss and Rosie hung round the door.

"What's that?" Lyndz whispered, pointing up to a dark shape hanging from the exposed beams of the ceiling.

"Dunno." Frankie went to inspect further. Then she went kind of pale and started to back out of the chapel.

"Bats!" she shrieked when she was by the door. "Loads of them!"

We started screaming and running all at the same time.

When we were back at the house we collapsed in our bedroom. Thank goodness we could lock the door this time – the locksmith had sorted out the problem.

"Everything adds up," I gasped. "The noises we heard, the cross, the bats. I reckon we did stumble upon some vampires the other night."

"Shouldn't we tell someone?" Fliss asked frantically.

"No way! Besides, I think Uncle Bob knows," I told them. "Remember how he told us to go to the chapel? Maybe he's testing us out. We've got to get ourselves prepared with crosses and stakes and go down there and slay ourselves some vampires!"

"Not tonight?" Rosie looked alarmed.

"Nope, tonight we've got another mission to accomplish," I reminded them. "Tonight we're going to scare Molly and Carli witless!"

You know when you're really up for something but you've got to wait for the right time to do it? Well, it's like time goes on strike, isn't it? Every minute just stretches out in front of you. Even listening to Uncle Bob's stories wasn't so much fun because we were so keen to get on with some action of our own.

We went to bed ahead of everyone else and ran through our plan one last time. Then it was just a case of waiting until Molly and Carli came upstairs before we could sneak out to the attic.

"What if Ben and Spike wake up? Mum might rumble what we're up to." Lyndz looked anxious. "And she's been so great since she's been here, I don't want her relapsing into one of her moods again."

"Look Lyndz, that's a chance we'll have to take," I said firmly. "We know where the boys' bedroom is – we'll just have to make extra sure that we don't make any sound when we walk over it. Ready?"

The others nodded. "Ready."

We wrapped ourselves in our dressing gowns and crept out into the passageway. The others crept towards the door leading to the attic and I went to Molly and Carli's room.

"Mum says you're to turn off your tape and go to sleep NOW!" I shouted through the door. "She's still mad with you about our bedroom door. And if you don't shut up she says you'll have to miss out on the party."

"You creep!" Molly yelled back, but within seconds she'd turned off her music and the lamps.

"We'd better do what the scumbag says," I heard Molly whisper. "She'll probably grass us up otherwise, and there's no way I'm missing that party!"

I put my thumbs up to the others and crept to join them.

Now I'm glad that we have torches as part of our sleepover kit, because we certainly needed them up there in the attic. It was so dark you just couldn't see anything in front of you. And cold too! Somehow it seemed so much bigger than it had done in the daytime.

"We must be there by now!" whispered Rosie. "Are you sure we haven't passed the packing cases we used to mark out Molly's room?"

"No way!"

"Listen!" Lyndz suddenly hissed. "Isn't that Spike crying?"

We all held our breath. If Lyndz's mum came to check on him, as sure as eggs is eggs she'd check on us too. Molly wasn't the only one who might be missing the party!

"It's OK, I think he must just be having a dream," Lyndz sighed with relief when there was silence below us again.

"Well at least we know that Molly's room isn't too far away," Frankie whispered. "Look, the cases are here."

We tiptoed to the middle of them and grinned at each other.

"Let's do it!"

Frankie and I took off our dressing gowns and started to drag them over the floor, making a loud swishing sound. Fliss and Rosie danced and stamped around whilst Lyndz moaned and groaned.

To begin with, we thought Molly and Carli must be asleep because there was no sound below us. Then we heard a low urgent murmuring. We stopped where we were, then started again – swishing, stamping and moaning. It was all going fantastically – until Lyndz's moans were joined by loud "hic!"s. She'd got the dreaded hiccups!

"No Lyndz!" I almost shouted, running over to her and clamping my hand over her mouth. "You'll give the game away."

By that time we could hear anxious sobs below us.

"Time we were gone!" I whispered to the others.

We hurried to the stairway as quickly and quietly as we could. Turning to the others I laughed, "Go on, tell me that wasn't our best yet!"

But no-one spoke. They looked terrified. I spun round to see what the problem was – only to be met by the shadowy figure of a man looming up the stairs towards us.

CHAPTER EIGHT

I took one look at the lumbering form and started to scream. I wanted to run back up to the attic, but my legs had turned to jelly.

"Away with your screaming," chuckled the figure, emerging out of the shadows. "Anyone would think you'd seen a ghost!"

"Uncle Bob!" we gasped in unison.

"You see!" sobbed Fliss. "He keeps appearing without us hearing anything."

"Fliss!"

"Well it's weird! And scary!"

But there was something much scarier coming up the main stairs – MUM! She was on the warpath, wanting to find out what all the commotion was about. Molly and Carli were outside their bedroom weeping and wailing about spooky sounds in the attic. Mum was bound to see us and put two and two together – she's very good at that kind of maths.

Uncle Bob motioned for us to hurry along the landing and closed the attic door behind us. As Mum rounded the corner, we were almost back outside our own bedroom.

"Ah, there you are, Valerie," he greeted Mum warmly. "I found these wee lassies terrified out of their wits. They say something has been making a proper din up there." He pointed to the attic. "It must be Headless Eric doing his rounds again. He's the house ghost; a noisy wee thing but he's harmless enough. Wouldn'ae hurt a flea."

Mum looked at us suspiciously so we tried to look as terrified as possible.

"D-did you hear it too?" Frankie stammered as Molly and Carli appeared, trembling and shaking. "Wasn't it gruesome?"

They both nodded, and it took me all my time not to burst out laughing. Respect to

Frankie, she played an absolute blinder. They were totally convinced that we really *had* been scared by Headless Eric!

"I'll hear no more talk of ghosts!" said Mum sternly, ushering us back to our rooms. "There must be a perfectly sensible explanation for the noises."

She stared hard at Uncle Bob as she spoke. He just carried on smiling, but as soon as her back was turned he gave me a great big wink and the cheekiest grin!

When Mum had finally gone back downstairs I nearly exploded.

"Isn't Uncle Bob just the most fun?" I grinned, tossing a handful of fizzy fish at the others. "I mean, how many other adults would have got us out of that mess?"

"He certainly is one barmy old dude!" agreed Lyndz, whose hiccups had disappeared in the excitement.

Fliss didn't say anything, she just sat on her bed chewing her sweet thoughtfully.

"But you were pretty awesome too, Frankie," Rosie reminded us. "Talk about thinking on your feet!"

Frankie stood up on her bed.

"I thank you all, my humble servants!" She bowed elaborately.

"No need to get carried away!" I said, thwacking her with my pillow.

We hadn't had a pillow fight for ages so the others joined in. Wicked!

Afterwards, as we lay exhausted on our beds, I told the others, "If we put as much energy into our vampire-slaying, those demons won't stand a chance!"

"Aw man, can't we have a break from all that?" Rosie moaned. "This holiday is turning out to be pretty exhausting."

"Look Rosie-Posie, we're on a mission," I told her firmly. "And we cannot fail."

I had intended to go on our vampire patrol the very next night, but we set out in the morning to do the touristy sightseeing thing and it was dark when we arrived back. However much we pleaded, there was no way that Mum was going to let us "roam about outside", as she put it.

The next day, party-frenzy hit town. We had

to help tidy up this room and help trim up that. And just when we thought it was safe to go outside, Uncle Bob got us to help move all the furniture around. Typical!

The same thing happened the following day too. As soon as the light was beginning to fade and we were about to head out of the door, Uncle Bob called us back.

"Ah there you are now," he chuckled. "I was hoping you'd be able to help me with these."

He produced a bag containing about a million balloons.

"We want the place looking nice and cheerful for the party, don't we now?"

"Couldn't we do that tomorrow, Uncle Bob?" I pleaded. "The party isn't until Saturday. We've still got two days left. "

"Ah now, there's all the cooking to do tomorrow, Kenny," he told me with a gleam in his eye. "And you don't want to miss out on the haggis-making, do you?"

He handed over the balloons.

"Kenny's the right one for that job!" Molly called out snidely as she and Carli walked past. "She's full of hot air!"

213

I could have strangled her. But Uncle Bob went one better – he made them dust all the books in his library! Classic!

"It's almost like your uncle doesn't want us to go outside, isn't it?" Rosie said, taking a breather from blowing up balloons. "Do you think he's got something to hide?"

"I don't know," I replied, thoughtfully. "But we're definitely going to find out tomorrow night."

In preparation for our vampire-slaying mission we went to bed early and made crosses from pieces of wood which we'd found in a box next to the fireplace in the lounge.

"Do you think these are going to work?" Fliss asked, holding up a very wonky-looking cross held together with Sellotape.

"Deffo," I assured her. "It's the *symbol* of the cross that vampires are scared of, it doesn't matter what they're made of."

I sharpened a few sticks as best I could with the help of Fliss's nail file.

"Look, I've got myself some stakes too! Bring on the vampires!"

But that night it wasn't vampires we had to deal with, but Headless Eric again. Or at least, that's what Molly and Carli would have liked us to believe. At about two o'clock in the morning I felt someone shaking me.

"Wassup!" I mumbled crossly. "Leave me alone will you?"

I looked up to see Fliss and Rosie staring at me.

"Listen!" Rosie whispered.

At first I couldn't hear anything. Then there was a scraping and moaning noise above us.

"It's c-coming from the attic!" Fliss stammered. "Do you think it really is Headless Eric?"

"Don't be daft!" I told her. "That was just Uncle Bob's story to get us out of trouble. It's got to be Molly, she must be stupid if she thought we'd fall for that trick ourselves."

"You mean she sussed it was us?" Frankie asked. She and Lyndz were now sitting on my bed with the others.

"Must have!" I shrugged. "Come on, let's go and sort her out!"

We crept to the door and out on to the

landing. We were halfway along to the attic door when all the lights were turned on.

"Sprung!" Mum announced viciously.

Molly and Carli were just in front. They looked absolutely amazed when they caught sight of us.

"Now I don't know who it was that rigged up that little charade," Mum was looking from me to Molly, "but it's beyond a joke. Nobody believes in ghosts, OK? And if there's any more mischief like that, you'll all be grounded and none of you will be going to the party on Saturday, is that understood?"

"But that's not f—" Molly began.

"*Is that understood*?" Mum repeated firmly.

"Yes!" We all nodded glumly.

"Now back to bed, all of you!" Mum watched as we headed back to our bedrooms.

As Molly passed behind us she hissed, "We'll get you back for that!"

"What did she mean?" Rosie asked crossly when we back in bed. "*They* were the ones pretending to be Headless Eric this time."

"I just want to know how they got back from the attic so quickly," Frankie yawned sleepily.

Hmm, that certainly was a mystery. But I could tap Molly for that information later. We only had one more chance to slay the vampires before we went home, and I was determined that nothing was going to mess that up.

All the next day we were as helpful as possible – fetching, carrying, peeling and chopping. We figured that if we worked our socks off all day, nobody could refuse us the chance to cut loose for a little while in the evening. And as we were in the kitchen I had the perfect opportunity to 'borrow' a little garlic – vampires *hate* that!

By late afternoon, the kitchen was groaning with food. There was just one last dish to prepare – haggis!

"What on earth is haggis anyway?" Fliss asked.

"Well," Mrs Barber grinned. "As Robbie Burns once wrote, it's the 'Great Chieftain o' the puddin' race'."

"Pudding, great! Count us in!"

Mum and Lyndz's mum exchanged weird looks.

"Well you'd better help me with the

ingredients then," Mrs Barber smiled, leading the way to the fridge.

Frankie took one look inside and dashed outside with her hand over her mouth.

"Gonna hurl!" she moaned.

Fliss and Rosie ran after her. Lyndz and I stayed to have a closer look.

"Och, the girl's gone soft. Has she never seen a sheep's heart and liver before?" Mrs Barber pretended to look amazed.

"And w-what's that?" Lyndz asked, pointing to another bloody-looking container lurking inside the fridge.

"Why that's the sheep's lungs!" Mrs Barber explained, removing the container. "And this here's the sheep's paunch, or stomach bag. We mix up all those goodies with oatmeal, onions and seasoning, then stuff it back in here and boil it. It's the most delicious thing you'll ever taste."

Lyndz had gone a funny shade of green. And I was feeling none too clever myself.

"Why don't you two run along and see if Frankie's OK?" Lyndz's mum ushered us out of the kitchen. "You've worked ever so hard today, go and get some fresh air whilst we finish up in here."

We didn't need telling twice. We ran and ran until we finally caught up with the others leaning against a tree outside.

"You OK?" I asked Frankie.

"Mm," she nodded. "It was all that bloody stuff, it was disgusting." She went pale again at the thought of it.

"You don't suppose your Uncle Bob really is a vampire himself, do you?" asked Rosie. "And that was the remains of one of his victims?"

Fliss squealed.

"Nah!" I shook my head. "But speaking of vampires, look it's getting dark. This might be our last chance to slay them. Let's go upstairs, grab our things and prepare to do battle."

We charged up to our room, stuffed the crosses, stakes and garlic into our pockets and ran outside again. Uncle Bob was just walking up to the house.

"You're brave venturing out there," he grinned. "You want to be careful, you never know what you might meet."

We all looked at each other and he went inside, rubbing his hands and chuckling to himself.

"There's something going on here and I don't l-like it," Fliss shivered. "Let's go back inside."

"Look Fliss, do you want to come with *us* or stuff disgusting muck into a sheep's stomach?" I asked her. "The choice is yours."

Felicity remained rooted to the spot.

"Felicity Proudlove, you are the weakest link, goodbye!"

We started to walk away towards the chapel.

"No, don't leave me!" she yelled and came hurtling after us.

"We'll be OK if we stick together," I told everyone firmly.

When we had the chapel in our sights we went in single file, creeping carefully and trying to make as little noise as possible.

As soon as we got to the chapel, we knew we were not alone. Something was moving about on the other side. Torches occasionally flashed, and there was a low murmuring of voices. I peeped through the open doorway and saw a hooded figure. I gasped and pulled back.

"There's something round the other side," I whispered to the others. "We'll have to creep round. It's too dark to go in here."

"I want to go home!" Fliss sobbed. "Please let's go back."

"I'm with Fliss," Rosie agreed. "Come on, this could be dangerous!"

My heart was pounding in my chest. And I admit that I was scared. Really scared. Part of me wanted to turn and run. But part of me thought: *Come on Kenny, this is exciting*!

Besides, I knew that the others would never let me forget it if they thought for one second that I was as terrified as they were.

"You stay here if you want," I hissed. "But I'm going in!"

I hugged the wall of the chapel as I crept stealthily round to the other side. Frankie was right behind me – I could hear her breathing down my neck. And Lyndz was behind her.

When we got to the corner I turned and whispered, "Get your stakes ready. On a count of three, let's get slaying. One, two, THREE!"

We rushed out like mad things, yelling and screaming at the tops of our voices. I executed a few high kicks, although at first I couldn't really see what I was aiming for, it was too dark.

Then I saw the figures again. There were lots more than I'd expected. I ran towards them with my cross raised, brandishing my garlic. I tried to do a flying drop kick just like Buffy, but it wasn't that easy. I seemed to get my legs all wrong and landed awkwardly. I tried to recover myself, but as I staggered to my feet something grabbed me from behind and dragged me into some bushes.

"Help! Frankie! Lyndz!" I yelled. But it was no good – *they'd got them too*!

CHAPTER NINE

"Leggoofme!" I yelled, thrashing about with my arms and legs. All I could see were these dark shapes surrounding me.

"Ouch!" I made contact with something, it felt like a shin. Whatever I'd kicked was obviously reeling in pain, so I tried more of the same.

"Och, you little wild beastie!" a man's voice snarled crossly. "Put the torch on her, Andrew!"

Now I'll admit that up until then, I was convinced that I was fighting for my life. We'd been captured by vampires who were going to kill us for sure. But that voice didn't sound as though it belonged to a vampire – and I'd certainly never heard of a vampire calling itself *Andrew*!

A bright light suddenly flashed on to my face. I blinked and tried to turn away from it. The first thing I saw was Frankie struggling furiously against two men who were holding her by the shoulders. Next to her a woman was grappling with Lyndz. They were all wearing jeans and anoraks. Now I know that vampires are masters of disguise – but *anoraks*? Per-lease!

"Just what on earth do you think you are doing?" asked the man behind me furiously. "Your silly games could easily disturb the bats and that's exactly what we're trying to avoid."

"Bats?" We all spoke together.

"Yes, we're here observing the bat colony in the chapel," said the woman. She was quite young and fortunately she didn't seem as cross as the other man. In fact she looked as though she was desperately trying to stop laughing.

"We've been here all week trying to establish approximately how many bats there are," she continued. "Whether they're in good health and how far advanced they are in their preparations for hibernation."

"Bats!" I repeated like an idiot. "We thought you were vampires!"

Everyone just cracked up. Talk about *us* disturbing the bat population! They made so much noise they probably disturbed every bat from Scotland to the South of France!

"Now, now. Don't mock the girls. I thought they showed great spirit!" Uncle Bob had appeared with Fliss and Rosie. They were all grinning from ear to ear.

"That was so funny!" Rosie was laughing so much she was almost choking. "You ought to have seen yourself, Kenny!"

"Can it, Rosie!" I snarled. "You knew about this all the time didn't you, Uncle Bob? Why didn't you tell us that there were bat-watchers here?"

"And spoil all your fun?" Uncle Bob grinned. "Now I couldn'ae do that, Kenny.

Look, no harm's done and now you're here you can watch the bats too."

He pointed overhead. The air was filled with black shapes sweeping out into the sky from the chapel. Once they'd soared higher, they seemed to swoop down suddenly.

"Eek, my hair! They'll get stuck in my hair!" squealed Fliss and put her hands protectively over her head.

"The last thing bats would do is land in your hair." The older man still sounded really annoyed with us.

"It's true," the woman told us gently. "They're swooping like that to feed on insects. They have to eat as many as possible at the moment because soon they'll be hibernating for winter so they're in the process of fattening up. Even these tiny bats can eat up to 3,000 insects at one feeding."

"Really?" I was totally stunned. "That's awesome!"

"But how can they see in the dark?" asked Lyndz.

"Well actually they don't," Andrew, the guy who'd flashed the torch in my face, explained. "They use a system of echo-location. That just means that as they fly, they make high-pitched sounds. They find out what obstacles are in their way by the echoes they get back. Clever, huh?"

"Wicked!"

"You know when I said I'd seen something flying past our window on the day we got here?" I told the others excitedly. "It must have been a bat! But I always thought bats were a lot bigger than these ones?"

"Oh they can be," the woman explained. "These are pipistrelles. They're the smallest and most common bats in Britain. They only weigh about seven grammes, tops."

"Wow!" breathed Frankie. "That's tiny!"

When we were sure that all the bats had left the chapel we crept to the doorway to take a peek inside. There was a faint high-pitched noise, coming for somewhere.

"Careful everyone," the man told us. "It sounds like there's a bat in trouble."

We shone our torches on to the beams and over the ground.

"Look!" Fliss suddenly whispered. She

shone her torch over to the far corner of the building.

There on the ground was a tiny bat. The man went over and very gently picked it up. You ought to have seen it. It was so tiny, and its wings looked far too big for it somehow.

"I think it's probably just hungry," the man said. "We'll take it back with us and have it checked over. My guess is that it'll just need feeding up. Then we can release it back here in a day or two. Would you like to hold it?"

Oh, man! I don't know why people think bats are so scary, they're just gorgeous, all soft and cute. It looked a weeny bit like my rat Merlin, only it was a lot smaller – and it had wings of course!

I thought that Fliss would rather have her hair chopped off than hold a bat, but I was wrong. After a little persuasion she held her hand out – and was totally smitten.

"Isn't it just so *cute*!" she kept squeaking. "You're just adorable aren't you, little batty!"

The poor guy had to virtually prise it off her so that he could put it in his special bat box.

"Ah, here you are!" Dad suddenly appeared. "Seeing all the bats really takes me back to my childhood, Bob. I remember coming here for the holidays and being absolutely fascinated by them."

"Dad! You *knew* about the bats and you didn't say anything?" I accused him.

"Sorry Kenny, I didn't think," he shrugged. "Anyway you lot, it's supper time. Come on then, look lively!"

I don't think any of us really wanted to tear ourselves away from the bats, but it was getting kind of chilly.

"How will we find out if the bat's all right?" I asked.

"Well, you can ask Gordon here tomorrow night." Uncle Bob slapped the chief bat-watching guy on the shoulder. "All my batty friends will be coming to the party!"

"Excellent!"

As we were saying our goodbyes, the woman asked, "How come you thought we were vampires?"

Hmm, good question.

"Well, we'd seen shapes when we explored

round the chapel earlier in the week," I began.

"And saw the torches and heard noises," Rosie continued.

"Then when we came back there were all these footprints," Frankie added.

"And we found this cross." Lyndz rummaged in her pocket. "So we thought, you know, someone was trying to fend off a vampire or something."

"My cross!" The woman's face lit up. "I knew I'd lost it here the other night but I never thought I'd find it again! This is brilliant!"

Lyndz handed the cross over.

"I'm Shelley by the way," she said. "It's been great meeting you guys. I'll bring some information on bats to the party if you like. There are probably some roosting near where you live. You could form a bat group of your own!"

"Cool!"

"Excellent idea!"

"Well, that was an unexpected way to spend the evening!" Frankie mused as we walked back to the house. "I'm kind of glad we didn't have to fight off any vampires though, aren't you Kenz?"

"Nah, I was well up for it. Ha-yah!" I launched into a manic kickboxing frenzy.

"That's not what it looked like to us," spluttered Fliss. "It looked like you were peeing your pants when that guy grabbed you!"

"Oh yeah!" I stopped and stood in front of them menacingly. "We'll see who pees their pants when we've got to eat that haggis at the party tomorrow!"

And with that rather gruesome thought we all ran screaming into the house!

CHAPTER TEN

Now, as you know, I am Kenny 'Party Animal' McKenzie, so I was well up for Uncle Bob's little shindig – especially as the house was trimmed up like you wouldn't believe. Besides the balloons and stuff we'd put up, Lyndz's parents had really gone to town with the decorations. They're both dead artistic. In fact Lyndz's dad is the Head of Art and Design at the Comprehensive back in Cuddington.

Uncle Bob produced tons of spare tartan material (don't ask why he had it, I don't know). As soon as Lyndz's mum saw it, her eyes lit up.

"This is marvellous, Bob!" she squealed. "We could decorate your home like it's never been decorated before. Hey Keith!" she called out to Lyndz's dad. "Come here and take a look at this!"

We all looked at each other and shrugged. I mean, maybe it's an adult thing, but I couldn't see what was so exciting about a bit of checked cloth! Anyway, Mr and Mrs Collins sat huddled over the table for ages, making loads of drawings. Then they set to work on the dining room and the lounge. They swathed tartan around the walls and draped it over the tables. It looked just amazing. And all the time they were doing it they were giggling like teenagers and sneaking the occasional kiss when they thought we weren't looking – gross! Poor Lyndz was so embarrassed she couldn't watch.

"Well, I think it's cool!" Fliss told her. "I mean, it's much better than your mum being miserable like she was before, isn't it?"

"Yeah, I guess!" Lyndz admitted.

The Sleepover Club did our bit with the

decorations for the party too. We made all these bat shapes and hung them up in the hall so they looked as though they were flying about.

"Great bats, girls!" Uncle Bob looked at them admiringly. "Or should that be 'vampires', eh Kenny?"

He started chuckling in that throaty way of his.

"Now girls," he continued. "I hope you won't be too tired by this evening. The dancing gets pretty wild in these parts, you know."

"That's just what we like!" I grinned, and we showed him just how wildly we can dance. Uncle Bob just stared at us with his mouth open. I guess it was a pretty scary sight.

"Do you want to borrow some of our tapes?" asked Frankie. "We've got all the top tunes: S Club 7, Hear' Say…"

"Well, that's very kind of you," he smiled, "but I have a band lined up. In fact I was just coming to welcome them. I saw their van coming up the driveway a minute ago."

"Excellent!"

"Who do you think it'll be?" asked Fliss excitedly. "What about Travis, they're Scottish aren't they? Or Texas?"

A *real band*! This was going to be amazing.

"Who are they? It can't be…" Frankie's voice trailed away as a group of elderly men were greeted warmly by Uncle Bob. They had various instruments with them – a couple of violins, an accordion, a flute, a huge drum kit and…

"Bagpipes?" we all gasped in horror.

"How can you possibly dance to bagpipes?" groaned Fliss.

And I have to admit that just at that moment, Uncle Bob's party sounded about as exciting as an evening of back-to-back news programmes on the telly.

"Look, we'll just have to make the best of it!" Lyndz said brightly when we were back in our room getting changed. "Everybody's gone to a lot of trouble for this party. And besides, it was great of your Uncle Bob to invite us up here in the first place. What would he think if we turned out to be a right load of moaning minnies, just because he's not having the music *we* like to dance to?"

Trust Lyndz to make us all see sense. And actually, we were way off-beam about the party anyway.

As soon as we got downstairs and mingled with the other guests, we started having a great time. Although we were just the *teensiest* bit under-dressed. All the men (including my dad and Lyndz's dad) were wearing kilts, and the women were wearing posh swirly tartan skirts.

"I told you we should have brought our best party clothes," Fliss hissed.

But Lyndz's mum came to the rescue when she provided us all with tartan sashes. At least when we put them on we didn't feel so left out (even though mine did clash with my football shirt!).

We'd been downstairs for a while when Shelley rushed up to us.

"I've been looking for you everywhere," she smiled. "I thought you might like these."

She gave each of us a bat badge and a great big information pack from the Bat

Conservation Trust. It looked really great, with special sections for people our age and everything.

"We'll definitely contact them," I promised.

"How's that little bat you took away?" Fliss asked her anxiously.

"Oh just fine!" Shelley reassured us. "Gordon was right, the poor wee mite needed feeding up. We'll probably bring him back tomorrow."

"Great!"

Suddenly a loud gong rang out from the hall.

"Ladies and gentlemen!" Uncle Bob announced very grandly. "Supper is served!"

Excitedly we followed everyone else through to the dining room and found our places. We were sitting with the bat watchers, which was pretty cool. Gordon, who had seemed such a misery-guts the previous evening, actually turned out to be a real laugh. He never stopped teasing us about being a vampire. He'd even brought some of those fangs you get from joke shops, and kept swooping over us pretending to bite our necks! In fact he was just pretending to ravage Fliss when the most appalling racket filled the air.

"Sounds like Headless Eric has met with another victim!" I whispered to Frankie.

"Don't be daft!" she chided. "It's the bagpipes!"

You'll never believe what happened next. It was awesome. First the piper came into the room playing his pipes, followed by Mrs Barber who was carrying – *the haggis*! Bizarre or what? Then it got even stranger when Uncle Bob started reciting "Ode to a Haggis" by some guy called Robbie Burns.

"Do they normally talk to their food like that?" Fliss asked, looking bewildered.

Actually we didn't understand a word of the poem, but everyone else seemed to know it by heart. But the absolute best bit was at the end when Uncle Bob got out this silver dagger and stabbed the haggis so that the steam burst out of it and its smell filled the dining room. It didn't smell too bad actually, but Frankie went quite green just thinking about what was in it. Now you know me, I usually try anything once, but I was with Frankie on this one. We just looked on politely as everyone else tucked in and washed it all down with 'wee drams' of whisky. (If you ask me, the whisky smelt worse than the haggis!)

"Now I didn'ae want to confuse anyone," Uncle Bob stood up, grinning. "This isn'ae January the twenty-fifth, so we're not celebrating Burns Night again. I just thought no-one would object to sharing all the pageant of one of our greatest celebrations with our wee Sassenach friends."

A loud cheer went up.

"But don't you bairns fret," he continued. "You're not going to go hungry. Bring out the feast, Mrs Barber!"

And what a feast it was! It was all authentic Scottish grub too. We had Scottish beef (well, Frankie didn't obviously) and mashed 'neeps and tatties' (mashed turnips and potatoes to you and me). And for pudding there was 'clootie dumpling'. I know it sounds weird but it was a fruity pudding. Gordon told us that it got its name from the 'cloot' or cloth it's wrapped in whilst it's cooking!

After we'd finished eating, one of Uncle Bob's cronies, Angus, stood up and recited another poem.

"Crikey! Are they going to go on like this all night?" Rosie wondered.

I know it sounds dead boring listening to poetry, but it wasn't at all. At least Angus's one was easier to understand. It was about this guy, Lochinvar, who ran off with someone else's bride or something. It was a bit gushy but Fliss loved it.

"Right everyone!" Uncle Bob announced at the end of the recitation. "Let the dancing commence!"

Cheering, everyone made their way into the lounge where the band was warming up.

Now, I don't know if you remember my efforts at line dancing when we had our Fun Day at Mrs McAllister's stables? Well, my attempts at Scottish country dancing were even worse than that! It was just so confusing! There were Scottish reels and jigs and dancing in squares. We 'Stripped the

Willow', performed 'A Highland Welcome' and danced something called, believe it or not, 'The Elephant Walk'! It was great fun and nobody bothered at all when we messed up. Poor Gordon though, I trod on his toes so many times he eventually announced that he was "retiring injured".

We danced for so long that I thought my legs were going to drop off.

"This is more exhausting than a soccer match!" I gasped, collapsing into a chair.

"You're not kidding!" agreed Frankie, flopping next to me. "I'm completely wrecked."

"Hey girls, have you any idea what time it is?" Mum was being swung wildly around the dance floor by Uncle Bob. She was kind of pink in the cheeks, but she looked as though she was enjoying herself.

"Yeah guys, it's almost midnight!" Dad came over to us. "We've a long drive ahead of us tomorrow and I want to make an early start. I'll be calling it a night myself soon."

I certainly was very tired.

"Are Molly and Carli going to bed too?" I asked.

"They've been in bed *ages*!" Dad laughed.

"Losers!" I grinned. "They just couldn't stand the pace, could they?"

We said goodnight to everyone and promised to keep in touch with Shelley. As we went upstairs Lyndz's mum and dad were spinning round together in the centre of a circle whilst everyone else clapped.

"What are they like?" Lyndz groaned. But you could tell that she was really chuffed that they both looked so happy.

We crashed out as soon as we got into bed. No midnight feast, nothing.

It was a huge shock to the system, having to get up early the next day. Not only that, but as soon as we'd had breakfast Dad was eager to be off.

"Thank you so much, Uncle Bob!" We all hugged him, before we piled into Lyndz's van. "We've had the best time ever!"

"Well, you're welcome to come back whenever you want!" he grinned warmly. "I can't guarantee you any vampires, but we have ghosts a-plenty in these parts!"

As we were driving off, Fliss said, "Do you

think there really *are* ghosts here? He seemed pretty serious, didn't he?"

"I don't know about ghosts, Fliss," Lyndz's mum piped up from the front. "But there's certainly magic in the air at Bob's place."

Lyndz's father smiled at her and she leaned over and stroked his cheek.

"Yukarama!" Lyndz moaned, and we all burst out laughing.

"You know, we never did ask Molly whether it was her and Carli who pretended to be Headless Eric that night," Frankie mused.

"That's right! We'll ask the slimy snake as soon as we stop," I promised.

And that's exactly what we did. But you know what? She just went very white and stuttered:

"W-we thought it was you!"

"What? That second time, when Mum turned on the lights?" I asked.

"Yeah. Mum told us that she thought you'd been having a laugh the night before. So when we heard the noises again we were coming to sort you out!" Molly explained. We could see by her face that she was dead serious.

"So if it wasn't you," Fliss squealed, "who was it?"

Now I don't know about you, but I have serious doubts about the whole thing. Part of me thinks that maybe it was Uncle Bob having a laugh. You've seen what a barmy old goat he can be. But part of me really believes it *was* Headless Eric spooking us out in the attic. I reckon we'll have to go back up to Scotland soon, to do some serious *ghost*-busting this time. What do you think?

IF YOU ARE INTERESTED IN BATS
CONTACT:

The Bat Conservation Trust
15 Cloisters House
8 Battersea Park Road
London
SW18 4BG

or check out their website at:
www.bats.org.uk

Sleepover Club Witches

by Jana Hunter

An imprint of HarperCollins*Publishers*

CHAPTER ONE

Come in, quick. Sit down. I've got something to ask you, and it's dead serious.

Have you got a sister? A crummy big sister? The kind who hates to see you having fun and always tries to ruin things for you? Have you ever wanted to put a spell on that jealous sister? You know, make her disappear, grow warts, or turn into smelly frog-slime and slither off down some deep well? I have, 'cos my sister Molly really messed up things for the Sleepover Club at Hallowe'en. And it wasn't funny (not at first, anyway). Mind you, when Frankie did her witchy thing and scared everyone half to death it was killing. The best. And when Rosie went haywire with the Curse of the Nerd's Nose, that was something else.

But that wasn't all.

There was Merlin (my pet rat) and his sneaky trail of rat's droppings. There was the candlelight and the secret chants and all the dark, dark, mysterious goings-on. Then there was the trouble I got into for stealing bits of Molly...

Why she had to make such a fuss about a teeny weeny bit of belly-button fluff, goodness only knows! But that's Molly for you. Always making a big deal. If only she was like my other sister, Emma. Emma's my oldest sister and she's all right, she is. Molly is different. Gruesome. Is it any wonder we call her Molly the Monster?

Look, I know I'm going on about Molly, but she nearly ruined our Sleepover Club, and that's the most important thing in the world to me and my mates, as anyone knows.

Wait. D'you want to hear everything that happened? I bet you do. Okay, here goes... It started on a Friday night. (That's our regular sleepover night, in case you don't know.) It was right before Hallowe'en and the Sleepover Club was getting in the mood for a specially *spellbinding* time (spellbinding... get it? spells, potions, witches and stuff). See, my four friends were due at my house any minute. We wanted to work on our trick-or-treat stuff before the dreaded M&Ms, Emma Hughes and Emily Berryman, beat us to it. The M&Ms are our biggest enemies at school and they were sure to have nasty tricks up their sleeves. The gang had some great sleepover things planned: costumes, tricks, witchy games and creepy ghost stories all topped off with the most wicked midnight feast of black sweets. We had liquorice, Black Jacks, Wine Gums, Fruit Pastilles, jellybeans, Black Imps and best of all, black Jelly Babies! It was going to be the most coo-ell sleepover in history! But of course, Molly the Monster didn't like that. Oh no. She had to create a scene the minute she heard about it.

"But *Mu-um*!" she whinged, stamping her silly foot. "Mum, you promised Jilly could sleep over next time we had swimming practice and it's swimming practice tomorrow!"

Mum clapped her hand to her forehead. "Oh no!"

Of course Molly had to take advantage of the look on Mum's face, by whining, "Kenny can't have our bedroom tonight, Mum. You promised!"

"I just didn't realise it fell on Kenny's sleepover night."

"She can have her baby sleepover tomorrow," said Molly. "Saturday."

"Saturdays are out while the Cuddington Ballroom Contests are on," sighed Mum. "I've got customers booked up for the next four weeks." (Mum does hairdressing at home, and while the Ballroom Contests were on she had glamorous grannies lining up to get their purple rinses and perms.)

"Our sleepover's tonight. The gang's already on their way," I protested.

"Mum promised me," Molly said in that annoying singsong voice she always gets when she thinks she's got one over me. "And anyway Jilly's on her way too... *with her mum*."

"Too bad the Sleepover Club got in first!" I retorted.

"Too bad for *you*, Laura McKenzie." Molly made a face at me. But she waited for Mum to leave the kitchen before she gave me one of her big, fat pokes. "Too bad 'cos I'm having my friend over to stay tonight no matter what. So you can forget your soppy Sleepover Club."

That did it.

How dare she call the Sleepover Club soppy? Our Sleepover Club is the best, the most brilliant fun in the world, and nobody calls it names. For a start it's got me, Kenny, in it (Laura McKenzie to people who want to get on the wrong side of me). But it's also got my best mate Frankie (Francesca Thomas) in it, so that makes it fantabulous, 'cos Frankie's a real laugh. Then there's Lyndz (Lyndsey Collins) the soft-hearted giggly one, Fliss (Felicity Proudlove) the sugar-and-spice one and Rosie Cartwright the most down-to-earth grown-up one, altogether the five most coo-ell girls in Cuddington School.

And we are not soppy!

That's why when Molly called us that, I had to get my own back by pretending to sigh a huge great sigh. "What a shame there won't be room for your dear little friend to sleep over..." I went. "I s'pose the only thing you can do is camp out in the garage.

'Course, you'll have to share your sleeping bag with Merlin..." Molly hates my rat more than a double dose of poison. "I'm sure Merlin would love to nibble your toes."

That put the King in the cake.

Molly went for me. I went for her. And in no time we were rolling about on the floor like those mad wrestlers you get on telly.

"Ooof!"

"Ouch!"

"*Aaargggh!*"

It was well good. And I was winning too, when Mum had to spoil it by coming back into the kitchen.

"Stop it you two! Stop it right now!"

"She started it..."

"*You* started it!"

"I don't care who started it. Just stop it, or else!"

So because Mum sounded like she meant business this time, my *dear* sister and I did what she said, although Molly had to carry on making dorky faces at me behind Mum's back.

"Now listen to me," Mum ordered. "I've just been on the phone to Mrs Thomas, and she says since it's an emergency the Sleepover Club can decamp over at Frankie's tonight."

"But everyone's coming here!" I couldn't bear to think of my spider and web decorations upstairs going to waste. "Mum, I've been decorating my room all afternoon."

"I'm sorry, Kenny," said Mum.

"So-rry," mimicked Molly, being her usual super-annoying self. But before I had a chance to thump her, I saw something that would shut her up good and proper.

I saw it loom up out of the dark and float eerily up to the kitchen window, like something out of a horror movie. A sight so gruesome, so horrible, that it sent shivers all the way down to my size three trainers. It was big. It was green. And it had wicked red-rimmed eyes.

"Aaaargh!" screamed Molly, seeing it for herself. "It's a witch!"

"A what?"

"*A witch at the window!*"

Sure it was a witch. But I wasn't scared. I wasn't shocked. Not me. I just opened my mouth and yelled at the top of my voice:

"*Frankie!*"

CHAPTER TWO

I raced to the front door, and yanked it open. And, with the force of a jet-propelled broomstick, the wicked witch herself fell across our hall floor in a heap.

"Come in!" I laughed as the rest of the Sleepover Club tumbled in on top of her. "Oh, I see you already did!"

"Heh, heh, heh..." cackled Frankie-the-witch, looking up at me from the pile of my friends. "Want a bite of my poisoned apple?"

"Save it for Molly," I said. "She deserves it." I helped Frankie with her pointed hat while the rest of the Sleepover Club tried to untangle themselves from the heap of sleeping bags, sweets, cuddly toys, pillows, bags and Hallowe'en costumes strewn across the floor.

"You look well ugly!" I told her, dead admiring.

"I know."

"Molly's face!" giggled Lyndz, crawling about the hall floor, collecting all the scattered sweets. "She thought it was a real witch come to cast a spell on her."

"No such thing," said Fliss in her usual bossy way, as she folded up her sleepover kit ultra neatly. Fliss is a bit scared of supernatural things and she tries to cover it up by acting superior. She's also a total neatness freak, in case you didn't know. "Hope you've not squashed my cake, Rosie," she fussed.

"Oops." Rosie, who's known for being a bit of a klutz, went red. "Let me check..."

"Don't bother, Rosie," I told her glumly. "The Sleepover Club's not stopping."

"What!"

"But it's sleepover night!"

"I know. It's over at Frankie's instead."

"Mine?" Frankie's voice sounded muffled behind her green plastic mask. "But we had it at mine last time."

"I know. Molly's messed everything up, as usual."

There were moans of "typical" and "what a Monster". But before we had a chance to think up any worse names for my meddling sister, the doorbell rang and the monster herself flounced out of the kitchen and pushed past me.

"Out the way, little kids," she said, shoving Frankie-the-witch rudely. "I'm having my friend to stay over now. So your baby sleepovers are numbered..."

"Oh yeah?"

"Yeah!"

"What d'you mean?"

Molly looked smug as she delivered her killer blow. "Jilly's staying here Fridays now. So the Sleepover Club's out!"

We all gaped at her. Then Frankie piped up:

"That's what you think! Our Sleepover Club has rights!" Frankie will always stand up for herself in a fight, especially if she's wearing witch's talons and a pointy hat.

"Rights for you load of babies? You must be joking!" sneered Molly.

"We're not babies!"

"Yes you are!"

"*No we're not*!"

As you can see, things were getting out of hand, and Total War probably would've broken out if Jilly's mum herself hadn't peeped through the letterbox.

"Hello," she said, in a friendly voice. "Anyone going to let us in?"

This was definitely not the moment to start fighting. So, still boiling, we decided to cool it and plot our revenge over at Frankie's instead.

Because something Had To Be Done.

It's not that we minded sleeping over at Frankie's for the second week running. Frankie's got a huge bedroom with extra bunk beds, so it's well nice having our sleepovers there. (And as Rosie said, a sleepover is a sleepover.) No, we didn't mind so much about staying at Frankie's. It's just that, as Frankie said, "It's the principle of the thing. If Molly starts messing up our sleepovers, who knows what will happen next?"

And the gang agreed.

That's why I did what I did. The horrible, hairy deed itself. I mean, no point in letting a fat, juicy spider go to waste is there?

Carting our stuff through the streets was brilliantly creepy. It was so dark and silent that Frankie-the-witch kept cackling and pretending to put a spell on the houses.

"Eye of newt, toe of bat,
Light of the full moon,
Get lots of sweets for Trick-or-treat...
'Cos we are coming soon!"

"Ooo, ooo..." I chanted, waving my hands. "We'll put a spell on you, if you don't!"

But Fliss, whose mum doesn't approve of spells and stuff, was not having any of this. "Why don't we practise our 5ive routine?" she said, ignoring our class act.

"Not now!"

"Why? We've got loads of room out here..."

"NO!"

'Course, in the end Lyndz, seeing that Fliss was desperate to get off the scary subject of spells and witches, saved her, as usual. Lindz loves to rescue things. If there was a flea drowning in her tea, she'd probably fish it out and give it The Kiss of Life. "Come on, you two," she said, doing a 5ive-type kick. "Fliss is right. We've got loads of room to practise our routine here."

So we gave in.

At least, we tried. We tried five times to dance down the street and sing like our current favourite boy band, but we were so loaded up with stuff it was impossible to do the movements properly. Frankie of course was determined to put some witchy bits into our routine, so she stuffed her rolled-up sleeping bag between her legs and pretended to fly on it down the street. She made us laugh so much our singing went warbly. It was well funny.

Rosie kept dropping things too. She couldn't dance two steps without offloading something. While she was picking up one thing she'd drop two, then three... In the end she just threw everything down in a pile and plonked herself on top. "I give up."

"Me too," said Frankie, unrolling her sleeping bag right there on the pavement as if it was the most normal thing in the world. "It's way past my bedtime." Then, cool as a cucumber, she climbed into her sleeping bag, pulled her pointy hat down to her nose, and pretended to go to sleep.

I told you Frankie was a laugh, didn't I?

Everyone cracked up and poor Lyndz was almost wetting herself. "Oh, stop, stop..." she gasped, clutching her stomach.

"Hey!" Frankie-the-witch stuck her long nose over the edge of her sleeping bag. "Can't a person get some sleep round here?"

That did it. On a silent signal, we unrolled our sleeping bags and laid them out, on the pavement, alongside Frankie. All of us except Fliss, Chief Inspector of the Dirt Patrol, that is.

"You'll catch a disease," she predicted darkly.

"Good. Then Molly will be in deep doom forever," I said, pretending to wash my face and brush my teeth before settling down for the night. "It's Molly's fault we've been thrown out on to the streets, anyway. I think we should get the papers to come and take a photo, then she'd really get it."

"Yeah," giggled Lyndz. "I can see the headlines now: "Sleepover Club Is Streets Ahead.""

We laughed, but Fliss was still in a flap, going on about us ruining our clothes. She's the only one in our gang who's into clothes and icky romantic stuff, probably because of her Barbie-doll looks. "Get up, ple-ease," she cried in the end. "I bet dogs have weed on that pavement..."

"Not at this luxury hotel," said Rosie, who was making a night table out of her flattened bag by neatly laying out her hairbrush, headband, toilet bag and diary.

"It's not a hotel."

"'Tis to us."

"Well, I'm not stopping," announced Fliss. "And you'll be sorry if you do!" And with that she grabbed her sleepover kit, and marched off down the street with her nose in the air.

"She'll be back," said Frankie without moving. Actually Frankie hadn't moved since she'd rolled over and pretended sleep. "Fliss can't bear to miss a sleepover."

"Maybe she's gone to tell the papers," I offered hopefully.

"Tell her mum, more like."

But Fliss wasn't doing either. In fact, she hadn't gone very far at all.

We went on wondering where she was for a bit, but there's only so much time you can waste worrying at a sleepover. So soon we were telling jokes and sharing black sweets, there on the pavement, as if it was the most normal sleepover in the world. And we got so carried away by our street camp-out that by the time the ghost appeared, Fliss was the last thing on our minds.

"Whhhhoooo-ooooo..."

"Omigosh it's...!"

"Hooo-whhooooo..."

"Quick!"

"Run!"

And in a crazy jumble of sleeping bags, trapped feet and panic, the four of us did the

Sack Race of the Century right up to Frankie's front doorstep, screaming loud enough to wake the dead.

CHAPTER THREE

Which only goes to prove, you can't keep a Sleepover girl down.

Fliss may be the world's most finicky fusspot but she can still play a wicked ghost when she wants. Frankie said it was the moans that made her so spooky, but I reckon it was the sleeping bag over the head. You should've heard our screams as we tried to bunny-hop our way over to Frankie's. Reckon the whole of Cuddington did. All the dogs in the neighbourhood went mad, barking and howling, especially Pepsi, Frankie's dog. Frankie's mum said we nearly gave her a heart attack.

Hey, have you ever noticed how screaming makes you starving hungry? It does, you know, because after the Sack Race of the Century everyone was ready for Round Two of the sleepover feast.

Luckily we had masses of stuff.

As well as all the sweets, we had almost-black sausages on sticks, Marmite sandwiches, black grape squash and Fliss's Black Forest cake. We laid everything out in the middle of Frankie's bedroom floor and made a magic circle round the edge of it with her stone collection. It looked dead good. Then we did a little witch dance around it, holding hands and chanting, "Feast, Feast, Feast..."

Pepsi went barmy, especially when Frankie held her paws so she could dance with us on her back legs.

"Ta-daa!" went Rosie. "It's Pepsi the doggie dance star!"

"Woof, woof!"

"Take a bow, Pepsi," said Frankie and Pepsi actually bent her daft black head.

"Woof! Woof, woof!" She *loved* it.

After that we got down to some serious

eating. When we'd demolished the lot, we flopped on the floor, stuffed, and told each other Hallowe'en jokes. They were daft, but they made you laugh. Here are some of my favourites:

Question: Why does a witch ride a broomstick?
Answer: Because a vacuum cleaner's too heavy.

Question: What's a witch's favourite computer programme?
Answer: Spellcheck

Question: What big, green and smells?
Answer: A witch's nose.

Good, aren't they? My very very best, favourite was:

Lovestruck witch to handsome prince: What do I have to give you to make you kiss me?
Prince: Chloroform!

That one cracked us all up.

Lyndz laughed so much she got the hiccups. "Hic! What a lovely surprise for the handsome prince when he came round!"

"Talking of surprises..." I said. "That reminds me."

"What?"

"Molly's in for a massive surprise tonight."

"What is it?"

"Tell us!"

I giggled. "A huge hairy spider, hiding in her pyjamas."

"*Wicked*!"

"Serves her right!"

Frankie put her witch mask back on. (She'd only taken it off so she could eat.) "Heh, heh heh. There came a big spider, that sat down beside her..." she cackled.

"A spider in your bed is so creepy," shuddered Fliss dramatically. "I'd just die!"

"A spider won't stop Molly messing up our sleepovers," Rosie pointed out. Told you Rosie was dead practical and down-to-earth. "We've got to do more than that to stop her."

"Rosie's right. Molly's got swimming

practice every Saturday 'til the school gala. We've got to stop her."

"We could snip the straps off her swimming costume," giggled Lyndz, who wouldn't really hurt a fly.

"Or drain the school pool," laughed Rosie.

But Frankie was deadly serious. "Why don't we put a spell on Molly?"

We all stared at her.

"Like what?"

"We could make her so allergic to water she comes out in boils!"

"Er..." I think Frankie was getting a bit carried away with that spooky mask.

"We have to do *something*, Kenny! Molly's trying to mess up our whole Sleepover Club."

Frankie was right about that, and I could see the others agreed. This *was* serious. If we didn't put a stop to Molly's tricks the whole club was in danger.

"We-ell..." I said in the end, "I could gatecrash her swimming session tomorrow."

"And do what?"

"Just swim." (Secretly I was hoping to find a way out of putting nasty spells on my sister, even if she did deserve it.) "I'm a better swimmer than Molly and that really gets her goat."

"Hmmm..." said Frankie.

"I can tell her I'll be there every Saturday unless she stops trying to ruin our sleepovers."

"Maybe..."

"They'll let me into the school pool 'cos I'm Molly's sister."

Frankie thought for a moment longer. "Okay, go to the swimming pool tomorrow... And Kenny?"

"Yeah?"

"Make sure you show Molly who's boss."

"*Right.*"

Next morning I got to Molly's school bright and early.

Outside it was cold and foggy, but inside the pool had that lovely warm, fuggy, chlorine smell. Mind you, I wasn't warm enough to jump in yet. Besides, it was so fogged with steam, I couldn't see Molly at all. So I just stood by the edge, covered in goose pimples, trying to make out one school swimming costume from another.

But that didn't stop Molly the Monster from coming up behind me and making me jump out of my skin. "What are you doing here?" she snarled.

"Mum said I could."

"Liar!" Dripping cold water on to me, Molly stuck her big, wet face into mine. "Mum's already after you for putting that spider in my pyjamas, you little — "

"Oh dear..." I went, all innocent. "Didn't you like my little Hallowe'en surprise, then?"

Molly turned purple. "Get out of here," she hissed. "This is *my* school pool and *my* swimming practice."

"You don't own it. I can swim if I want to..." I began.

Molly's face was awful. "Go on then," she snarled. "*Swim!*"

And she pushed me so hard, I toppled and fell backwards into the pool... *splat!*

The water hit me across my shoulders like a steel whip and sent shock waves down my body. Down and down I went, gulping and kicking like mad. It was horrible. Horrible and nasty and scary and it seemed to go on forever. It was so bad that when I finally bobbed up, spluttering and gasping for air, I was determined to do one thing.

Beat Molly. As soon as Molly's team was ready for the three-length race, I got into position in an empty lane. No one even noticed me.

They soon would.

When the swimming instructor blew his whistle, I pushed my feet against the side of the pool with total force, and swam and swam as fast as I could. One two, one two, kick, kick, kick. Dip head, lift-and-gasp, swim, swim, swim. Faster, faster, faster. One length, dive-down touch and turn, swim, swim, swim. One length, two...

From somewhere far off there was a muzzy shouting, but my head seemed like it was in another place and time. I swam and swam, fast, faster, faster.

I cut through the water with my arms, kicking hard with my legs, right on to the end... *and made it in second place.*

YES!

Second place, beating Molly by one! You should've seen her face! The school swimming instructor was dead impressed (even if I wasn't supposed to be in the race). "What a shame you don't go to our school," he smiled, when I'd explained who I was. "We could use someone with your speed."

"Thank you, sir."

"Now, young lady, will you let us get on with our practice?"

"Yes sir."

He didn't seem to mind a bit that I'd joined in their race. In fact he was really nice.

As I made my way to the changing rooms, I felt so mixed up and funny, it was weird. I was proud and worried at the same time. Proud because of coming second and worried because of Molly's jealousy. But there was one thing I wasn't mixed up about.

Molly.

She'd come third in the race when I'd come second. And that could only mean one thing.

War.

CHAPTER FOUR

"Laura! Is that you?"

Uh-oh. Mum didn't sound best pleased.

"Can't stop, Mum! I only came to pick up something..."

"*Laura*! Come in here." Even with a mouthful of roller clips Mum could sound fierce. "I want a word with you, my girl."

I poked my head round the kitchen door. Phew! Mum was in the middle of doing a glamorous granny's hair and she'd never tell me off in front of a customer...

Famous last words.

Not only did Mum have a real go at me, but

her customer, Mrs Bramley, joined in too. The interfering old granny tut-tutted and nodded 'til every roller on her blue-rinsed head *shook*.

It was well humiliating.

"Fancy spoiling Molly's swimming practice! I'm surprised at you, Laura. And as for planting a spider in her bed..." Mum went on and on. She used words like 'sneaky' and 'mean' and, worst of all, 'disappointed'. My mum can make 'disappointed' sound the ugliest word in the world.

Then she dropped her bombshell.

"So you can forget sleepovers here, my girl."

"WHAT?!"

"Anyone who can wilfully spoil her sister's sleepover doesn't deserve to have her own!" Mum jabbed a roller clip into Mrs Bramley's scalp so hard, the glamorous old granny flinched.

"*Ouch!*"

"Sorry, Mrs Bramley."

"Mum... Mum, you can't stop sleepovers!" I began.

"Oh, can't I?"

"In *my* day we did what our mothers said..." Mrs Bramley muttered, rubbing her sore head.

"Please, Mu-um! Please, please, pleeease..."

"One more word and I'll get *all* sleepovers banned," warned Mum. "Molly said it, and the more I think about it, the more I see her point..."

"S-said what?"

"That it's on sleepover nights when the trouble starts."

A cold shiver went through me then. Now I knew what Molly was up to. She was trying to get the Sleepover Club banned *for good*.

"It's not fair!" I burst out. "Not fair!" And in floods of tears, I raced up to the bathroom and locked myself in for a good cry.

It wasn't fair. How could I explain to Mum that the reason I went to Molly's swimming practice was to stop the gang from casting a spell on her? All my good turns end up with me in trouble. Nobody appreciates me.

I don't know how long I stayed there, sitting on the lid of the toilet, bawling my eyes out. All I know is I used up a whole toilet roll. Then, just as I got to the dry-eyed and puffy-faced stage, I heard something through the bathroom wall. Molly the Monster and Silly Jilly were in the bedroom talking. And Molly sounded worried...

"If goody-goody Robin Hughes has his way, Chess Club will meet Saturday mornings! What'll I do about swimming practice then?"

"Well you can't do both. You're in the Chess Club Tournament."

"I know. Robin Hughes is such a nerd," moaned Molly. "He's sure to get his way."

"Yeah. The teachers love him."

"Like all the Hughes lot. His rotten cousin, Emma, is in my rotten sister's class."

Robin Hughes was one of the dreaded M&Ms' cousins! That was a hot piece of news. But hot or not, Jilly's next words made me go cold.

"Your rotten sister's gonna go ballistic when she finds out about her rat..."

Merlin! My lovely soft, twitchy-nosed pet. What had they done to him? I leapt up and stormed into the bedroom, puffy-faced and panting.

"WHAT HAVE YOU DONE WITH MERLIN!?"

The two conspirators looked up guiltily.

"WELL?"

Molly gave a slow shrug. "We never touched him." But I could tell from the smirky, sneaky way she slid her eyes over to Jilly, that something was up.

In a blind panic, I raced to the garage where I kept Merlin.

Please be all right, Merlin, I prayed. Please be all right.

But the door to my pet's cage was open, and his dear little home was empty.

Merlin was gone.

CHAPTER FIVE

Merlin was gone.

I searched and searched everywhere, but my sweet little pet was nowhere to be found.

Of course, Molly the Monster denied everything. But when my mum questioned silly Jilly, she couldn't keep it up. The sneaky creep admitted she'd opened the cage just 'to stroke Merlin' (I'll bet!) and that's when he'd shot out.

Molly, you Monster, you were behind this, I fumed to myself.

Jilly would never have gone into the garage if you hadn't told her to 'cos you're too weedy to touch Merlin yourself. But you planned his escape to get back at me.

That did it.

Determined to pay Molly back, I got on my bike and took off. Fast as a wild witch on a broomstick, I flew down the road to Cuddington library. And I found just what I wanted...

A book on spells.

Back at Frankie's, the rest of the gang was lazing about, watching telly and eating popcorn. They were enjoying the Sleepover Club's usual Saturday treat of swooning over our fave boy bands. Mind you, I could tell Frankie was ready for a distraction.

"OK gang, gather round," I said, spreading the *The Good Witches' Guide to Spooky Spells* open on Frankie's bedroom floor. "We've got Hallowe'en to prepare..."

"Wh-what are you going to do?" asked Fliss nervously.

"Learn how to make spells."

"Oh no..."

"Oh, YES!" I declared.

"We won't hurt anybody, Fliss," Lyndz promised.

"All we're doing is reading about spells," said Frankie, leafing through the book. "It's not as if we're going to turn anyone into a toad or anything."

But Fliss wasn't convinced. She went on and on about what her mum would say, and how we'd get into trouble (even though we all knew it was really because she was scared). Fliss can be such a wuss. Just the same, we weren't going to force Fliss to join in. Our gang is too hot on the rights of kids for that. So while we read up about wands and witches' broomsticks, Fliss got busy with an ordinary broomstick and cleaned up our sleepover mess from Frankie's bedroom. (That kept old Fusspot happy!)

What we read was dead interesting. How witchcraft didn't have to be evil, but could be about good magic and making things better. There was even a Good Witches' Code and we all pledged to follow it, to the letter. Learning the right way to do things was really important.

The Good Witches' Code

1. Do not wish harm on others.

2. Keep matches, oils and candles out of reach from little ones.

3. Get permission to light candles. Never leave candles unattended. Keep lit candles away from curtains, paper etc – anything that may catch fire.

4. Take a friend when out collecting material for spells. Don't go anywhere dangerous and let a responsible adult know where you plan to go.

5. Don't do any spell that means getting into a bath when you're tired. You might fall asleep!

6. Know your plants – which are poisonous, and which are endangered species – before you pick them.

7. Do not apply essential oils directly to the skin, without proper dilution.

8. Never drink or eat any of the ingredients to any spell.

9. Do not wear floaty sleeves or trailing clothes for casting spells, in case of accident.

10. Whatever you attempt, GET PERMISSION FIRST!

We were so engrossed in spells and shells, potions, lotions and charms, that I almost forgot my troubles.

Almost.

Merlin and the danger the Sleepover Club was in bubbled away inside me like a witch's cauldron. Bubble, bubble, bubble.

"Fliss, you'd like this one," said Lyndz, pointing to *Fairy Luck*. "You make a magic wreath of ferns and ivy sprayed with rosewater and hang it on your front door."

"*If* you want fairies to come," scoffed Frankie.

"I think it's sweet," Fliss sighed in spite of herself. "Getting all the little fairies to dance around at the bottom of your garden." Then she did a little ballet dance just to prove it.

Frankie gave a snort of laughter. She quoted from *Peter Pan*, "If you believe in fairies, just clap your hands!"

We all clapped like mad just for a laugh. Then Frankie did a wicked imitation of Peter Pan whooping and flying across the sky, I mean room. So me and Lyndz did an Indian Braves war dance on the beds while Rosie pretended to be Captain Hook. (Guess who had to be Tinkerbell?)

We had an ace pillow fight between the Indian braves and the pirates, then we went back to our spellbook.

When we got to the section on spells for *Harmony in the Home*, Rosie got thoughtful. "I'd really like to cast one of these spells," she said, all wistful and sad. "My house is such a tip."

Rosie's home was a bit of a mess. Her dad's in the building trade and when he split up with her mum, he left the house like a builders' yard.

"I think these spells are about harmony in the family. Not DIY," I pointed out gently.

"We could do with family harmony too," sighed Rosie.

I reckon Rosie hoped her dad would come back home and the family would be happy together again (even though her mum's got a new boyfriend). Personally, I think dear old Rosie-Posie was dreaming.

"I'm going to do a spell for Pepsi to have pups," said Frankie, who was desperate for more pets. "There's one here for babies, so I don't see why it can't work for dogs."

"Shame you don't need a sister any more," I said. "You could've had mine."

Frankie pulled a face. "No thanks!"

We all laughed. Frankie used to be a poor, lonely, only child always wishing for a sister. Now she had Izzy so she'd got her dream. It meant for once, Frankie had something in common with Fliss, whose mum had twin babies.

"What about you, Fliss?"

"We-ell, I *would* make a spell for this wonderful outfit I've seen in *Designer Fashions* but..." Fliss, who had turned her favourite colour of pink, trailed off.

"I'm going do a horse spell!" announced Lyndz. "For a horse of my own."

Frankie's reply rhymed: "A horse, of course!" She gave a loud neigh, "Neeeeeeigh..." and pawed the air.

We all fell about laughing, so Lyndz got up and did a noisy gallop round the room, jumping over our sprawled out bodies as if we were fences. Naturally Frankie had to raise the stakes by sticking her bottom in the air even higher.

"And it's Lyndsey Collins on Merrylegs, coming up to the final fence," Lyndz announced, pretending to rear at the sight of Frankie's bottom stuck up in the air.

Suddenly 'Merrylegs' threw back her head, snorted and took a running gallop at Frankie.

"YES!!!" we cheered as she sailed through the air.

"Neeeeeeigh!" 'Merrylegs' whinnied as she bashed into Frankie's bum.

"Watch out for the other riders!" I yelled.

"Aaargh!" We ended up in a heap in the middle of the room, rolling about and kicking like stallions.

It was well funny. But it couldn't make me forget that Merlin was still missing. It couldn't stop me worrying about him, and it couldn't stop me thinking about what I had to do.

"I'm gonna put a spell on Molly the Monster," I announced at last.

"Yay!" cheered Frankie.

"You can't wish hurt on another," Fusspot Fliss reminded me.

"Who said I would?" I mumbled rather feebly.

"Fliss, we have to stop Molly from ruining our sleepovers," said Frankie. "What kind of a spell are you going to put on her, Kenny?"

"A Love Potion."

"A Love Potion?!" My mates all gawped.

"Yeah," I grinned. "For my dear sister Molly to fancy someone like mad."

"Uh-oh," said Rosie. "Remember what happened last time…"

Rosie meant the time we tried to get a boyfriend for Brown Owl and we all got into trouble. Big Time.

"This is different," I went.

"How?"

"It's not for grown-ups."

Fliss, the one who loves *lurrve* so much she even marries her toys, was dead excited. "Who? Who will Molly fancy?"

"Are you sure you want to know?" I teased her.

Fliss thwacked me. And she was so keen to know my secret, she even forgot to be afraid of spells.

"The M&Ms' cousin," I said. "Robin Hughes, *the nerd.*"

CHAPTER SIX

Payback time! Just you wait, Molly McKenzie!

In order to make a spell for Molly, I had to gather as many bits of her as possible. Altogether I needed:

1. Nail clippings
2. Strand of hair
3. A shred of fluff
4. Red wax candle
5. Nail (the other kind of nail)
6. A teaspoon of rainwater
7. A fingerprint from subject's 'love object'

With a bit of know-how, it wouldn't be too hard to get a nail clipping or a hair or two. Trouble was, how was I supposed to get a fingerprint from Molly's 'love object'?

There had to be a way.

I thought and thought about it the whole of Sunday. I thought about it as I searched and searched for Merlin (and didn't find him). I thought about it as I scarfed down roast beef, Yorkshire pudding and a double helping of apple crumble. And I thought about it in bed. But, all I could think of was kidnapping Robin Hughes, and I didn't fancy that. I mean, what would we do with him, when we got him?

Then, just as I was about to fall asleep, it came to me! An idea so coo-ell, so ace and top, I nearly jumped out of bed.

At school on Monday, I told Frankie about my brainwave.

"Brillo!" Frankie gave me a high five. "Kenny, you're a star."

"You said it," I beamed. Frankie catches on quickly.

At break the two of us put the first part of the 'Love Potion Plan' into action. It relied on the M&Ms' love of meddling, so no problem there! But it also meant following the horrible pair, known as the Goblin and the Queen, into the girls' toilets at break. (The things we do for the Sleepover Club!)

We waited until the M&Ms were safely locked in the two end toilets. Then all we had to do was pretend to be having a private little chat, so that our enemies could accidentally-on-purpose overhear us.

"Frankie..." I began in an extra loud whisper.

"Yes, Kenny?" hissed Frankie.

"You know, Robin Hughes is gonna die if he hears my sister Molly fancies him!"

Frankie stifled a laugh. "Yeah. Robin mustn't *ever* find out that Molly's mad for him!"

"Exactly." I gave Frankie a huge wink. "It would ruin things Big Time for the Sleepover Club, if those two got together."

Stage One done. Cool as cucumbers, Frankie and I sauntered out of the girls' toilets. It didn't take long. We knew our trick had worked when the M&Ms went into one of their major heads-together whisperings in the corner of the playground. Those two love the chance to ruin things for the Sleepover Club.

And just to prove it, they did something only the M&Ms could do. It was in Arts & Crafts. Our class was doing Hallowe'en collages to decorate the classroom walls. We had orange and black paper, beads, fabric scraps, lots of autumn leaves, acorns and stuff and gallons of glue. Everyone was busily cutting and sticking, when suddenly Frankie burst out, "Wow! Just what I need for my spell for Pepsi's pups!"

"What?"

"Pearls!" Frankie pounced on an old string of fake pearls, which were tangled up with the ribbons and yarn. "The Baby Spell calls for pearls..."

Baby Spell!

Emma Hughes' eyes nearly popped out her head. Wow! Did she and her stupid partner go into a major heads-together thing this time! But it wasn't until clean-up time that we found out what they'd been up to. We were in the middle of cleaning up when Mrs Weaver said sternly, "Francesca Thomas, come out here."

The Goblin shot a look of triumph at the Queen. Frankie got up slowly and went over to Mrs Weaver's desk. "Yes, Miss?"

"I hope you haven't been stealing school property, Francesca," Mrs Weaver said severely. "You know how wrong that is."

Frankie flushed. "Yes, Miss... I mean, no Miss. I..."

"Have you taken something, Francesca?"

The class went dead silent. So silent you could probably hear my heart thumping in the stillness! But Frankie didn't answer.

Suddenly Mrs Weaver's voice cut through the silence. "Francesca," she ordered. "EMPTY YOUR POCKETS!"

Lyndz whimpered. Rosie clasped her hands. And Frankie turned all colours of the sun. My best friend hung down her head, then started to empty her pockets. One by one, she took out her secret private stuff:

One squirrel with a chipped tail (from miniature ornament collection)
One silver moon earring

One half-eaten packet of bubble gum
One used paper hankie
One dog biscuit with crumbs
A bit of pocket fluff
One 2p piece
A scrap of pink ribbon

Everyone craned their head to inspect the evidence.

"I-I just took this ribbon from the bin, miss..." Miserably, Frankie held up the crumpled scrap of pink ribbon. "Someone had thrown it away, so I thought it was OK...."

Mrs Weaver coughed. "Oh. Oh, I see."

Another *long* silence.

"Miss, are these what you're looking for, miss?" I said finally, holding up the pearls that Frankie had put back in the collage box.

The M&Ms gasped.

Frankie threw me a grateful smile and Mrs Weaver turned the same colour as Frankie's ribbon.

"Oh! Oh, yes. Thank you, Laura." Then smiling ever-so sweetly at Frankie, Mrs Weaver said, "All right Frankie, you can sit down now."

Whew! Frankie was innocent. Nobody but the M&Ms could ever have thought different.

Even so, it didn't stop Frankie from feeling just awful.

"It was as if I'd committed the major crime of the century," she shuddered. "Standing up there, in front of the whole class…"

"But you hadn't done anything," Lyndz comforted her. "And Mrs Weaver knew it."

"Those M&Ms…" muttered Rosie, shaking her head. "When will their meddling stop?"

"Not yet, I hope!" I snorted.

"Why? What d'you mean, Kenny?" asked Rosie, puzzled.

"If I get my way, the M&Ms' meddling is going to help save the Sleepover Club!"

"Huh?"

"Tell us, tell us!" begged Lyndz.

I looked at Frankie. She looked at me. "Tell them Kenny! Tell them!"

So we let the gang into our plan. How Frankie and I made sure the M&Ms overheard us. And how they were bound to set up Robin Hughes with Molly, just to foil us.

"Once Molly thinks someone likes her, it

won't matter whether she thinks he's the biggest nerd in the world, the flattery will go to her head. She's sure to choose Chess Club to be near Robin Hughes," I finished.

"I know Robin Hughes," announced Fliss importantly. "He lives round the corner."

"That could come in very useful," I said thoughtfully.

"But how will Molly fancying Robin Hughes help the Sleepover Club?" persisted Rosie, who could be a bit slow on the uptake sometimes.

"Well, if she's not going to swimming on Saturdays any more she won't need Silly Jilly to sleep over."

"So...?"

"So that means she won't need to get our sleepovers stopped."

"She'll be too busy with her new boyfriend to worry about ruining our club," explained Frankie.

"Excellent!" cheered Lyndz and Fliss.

"Brillo!" Rosie had to agree.

I huffed on my fingertips and rubbed them on my school sweatshirt. "Thank you, gang. How clever of you to notice!"

Now all we had to do was wait. The M&Ms would take care of the next bit for us, for sure.

Thank you, M&Ms... Thank you for helping us save our Sleepover Club!

CHAPTER SEVEN

Fliss was in heaven. "Ooh, look at these!" she sighed. "And these, and these!"

It was half term and we were in Harmony Heaven getting all the stuff for our spells. There were lotions and potions, mirrors, silver trinkets and tinkly glass wind chimes everywhere. The place was like Aladdin's Cave.

Rosie was sorting through the same basket of shells Fliss was sighing over. "You can almost see through this one," she said.

"Ooh! Perfumed candles!" gushed Fliss, rushing over to a glass shelf loaded with goodies.

Frankie, rolled her eyes. "How *romantic*!"

Ignoring Frankie's teasing, Fliss was now going mad on all the smelly stuff. "My mum would love these!" she said as she sniffed a packet of bath salts. "She's up all night with the twins' teething."

Just as I was thinking that Fliss's houseproud mum needed more than bath salts to make *her* relax, Lyndz ran up. "Look!" she said excitedly. "A bottle of coloured sand. My spell says that all I have do is sprinkle sand on the ground, and write 'Merrylegs' in it!"

"What for?"

Lyndz thwacked Frankie. "To get my dream horse, Donkey Brain!"

"Neeeeigh!" whinnied Frankie, remembering our last horsey game.

"Brrrrr!" Lyndz snorted back, and she reared just like a horse.

"Go for it, Merrylegs!" I cheered and Lyndz pawed the ground. But when she pretended to write 'Merrylegs' with her 'hoof', she knocked over a basket of novelty sponges and a plaster mermaid.

We scrabbled on the floor, collecting seahorse

and fish-shaped sponges, in total hysterics. But our laughter died a sudden death as the shopkeeper marched over. "Are you girls planning on making a purchase?" she demanded, waving her jangly bracelets in the air.

"Er…"

"We were…"

"We were just *horsing* around," Frankie finished, and before I could stop it, a snort of laughter had escaped from behind my hand.

The shopkeeper swelled up. "Young lady, if you're going to be rude…"

"Sorry," I cut in. "We're really sorry. And… and I do want to buy something." I stroked a red candle against my cheek. "I'd like this for my… *Lu-u-rve* Potion."

Uh-oh. Everyone got the giggles big time now. The only one who didn't find it amusing was you-know-who.

Shopkeepers hate kids.

So, after we bought what we needed for our spells, we agreed to boycott her stupid shop just to show her.

We did much better collecting pebbles in the White Swan pub's driveway. The man who owned the place was dead friendly. "Make a wish for me," he grinned. "To win the Lottery!"

"No problem!"

Things were going great. We had our candles, our shells, our sand and our pebbles. Now all we had to do was go to the Arboretum to collect twigs for wands.

The Arboretum is this huge tree park smack bang in the middle of Leicester. It's peaceful and green and has every kind of tree you can think of. We had no trouble finding the ones s'posed to have magical powers, hazel and rowan.

"Look at this." I rubbed the grey bark of a hazel tree. "You can tell it's magic."

"Only take twigs from the ground," cut in Frankie just as I was trying out a magic chant. Frankie collected signatures with her mum for 'Save a Tree' once and it's made her a bit bossy about living things.

"We care about the environment too, you know," I protested.

But my promise didn't stop Fliss the-ever-nervous-one from going, "Watch out no one sees us."

"We're not doing any harm," Lyndz consoled her.

"Heh, heh, heh!" I gave a wicked witch cackle. "That's what you think!" And waving my hazel wand about, I chanted:

"Eye of newt, slimy toad stew...
Time to put a spell on you!"

Cackling evilly, I chased the gang round the Arboretum threatening to turn them into frogs. It was well funny.

The gang went mad, and Frankie went haywire as usual. She raced round the trees and slid on her bum down the grass slopes yelling, "A witch! A witch!" Rosie nearly wet herself.

We were all shrieking and running like wild things, when suddenly Fliss stopped dead in her tracks.

"L-look over there," she panted, pointing to a boy the other side of the grass.

"Where?" We looked.

"It's Robin Hughes!" Fliss gasped.

We all looked at a tall skinny boy standing

under a tree taking notes.

"So *that's* my future brother-in-law!" I joked.

"Only if your spell works," laughed Frankie.

Robin Hughes, who was more like Harry Potter than Harry Potter himself, looked up from his notepad and blinked at us through his glasses.

"Robin!" shouted out Fliss. "This is Molly's sister. She's got a message for you!"

The poor boy went white.

"You know, Molly who's in the chess tournament?" I added.

"D-do you mean M-Molly M-McKenzie?" Robin stuttered.

"Yeah," I said as I ran up to him. "Hasn't your cousin Emma told you about her?"

"Well… yes, actually," said Robin, looking dead embarrassed.

"My sister says she wants to know when it's Chess Club. She really wants it to be Saturday."

"Oh," said Robin looking relieved. "Tell her it's going to be on Saturdays then."

Now it was my turn to feel relieved. If Chess Club was on Saturdays, the Sleepover Club might be out of danger!

But just to make sure I said, "Molly *really* wants to see you."

Robin went red. "Really...?"

There was an awkward silence. Then Robin seemed to screw up all his courage. In a sudden rush, he blurted out, "Tell her I'll see her there!"

(YES!)

"OK."

"See ya, Robin!"

"R-right."

Heh, heh, heh... Our little plot was working.

CHAPTER EIGHT

"Let me clean the bath, Mum!" I grabbed the Ajax and Mum's jaw dropped a mile.

"Thank you Kenny," she said, trying to act like it was the most normal thing in the world for me to offer to clean the bath after Molly the Monster. (I don't *think* so!)

Mind you, Mum wasn't the only one surprised at me lately. Believe it or not, in the last two days, I had sorted laundry, tidied Molly's side of the bedside table (even though Molly throws away anything of mine that goes on to her side) and cleaned her yucky hairbrush.

How else was I supposed to collect bits of Molly's horrible grunge for my witchy spell? But even a magical person has limits. When I had to fish out a bit of her horrible toenail from the bath, I almost threw up.

Molly the Monster had taken to having long, private baths ever since I gave her Robin's message about Chess Club. She didn't fancy him (*yet!*) but even a nerd showing interest in you is better than no one. So with Saturday looming, my gruesome sister was probably trying to decide which club she'd go to – swimming or chess. The suspense was killing me!

But that wasn't the only thing looming. Hallowe'en was next week. The thing was, we'd got fab stuff planned for our Hallowe'en sleepover, but so far we had nowhere to have it.

Every parent had said a big fat "No".

See, the ugly rumour that our Sleepover Club was 'trouble' had spread. Jilly's mum was friendly with Lyndz's mum and the two of them had a real downer on us (all Silly Jilly's doing, of course). They were forever on the phone, complaining about things the gang got up to at sleepovers. And as soon as the other mums got wind of this, they started being mardy about sleepovers too.

True, with all my cleaning, my mum was definitely softening… But there was no way she'd go back on her word to ban sleepovers at our house. Not yet, anyway. When even Mrs Thomas gave a weak excuse, things looked desperate.

So the Sleepover Club had a conference call.

A conference call is where phone lines are linked up so different people can speak together at the same time. Here's how it works with our gang.

We've all got mobiles now, amazingly. First, I call Frankie on our home phone. Next, Frankie answers me and calls Lyndz on her mobile. Then Lyndz answers on her home phone and calls Fliss on her mobile. Fliss answers on her mobile and calls Rosie at home. Finally Rosie calls my mobile on her mobile. Hey presto! We're linked in a big circle! We each hold a home phone at one ear and a mobile at the other and we talk! It's dead cool!

"We've got to stop that Jilly coming over to your house," said Frankie into both her phones. "She's winding all the mums up."

"Yeah," Lyndz and I said together.

"Lyndz, ask Fliss how her campaign to get Robin Hughes interested in Molly is going."

If the plan to get Molly preoccupied with Robin Hughes didn't work, she'd carry on ruining our Sleepover Club. I could hear Lyndz talking to Fliss and I waited for her to give me Fliss's answer.

"Fliss says she 'accidently-on-purpose' bumped into Robin on his way home from school. She went on and on to him how *nice* Molly McKenzie was."

"Yuck! How did he act?"

"Just looked puzzled, Fliss says."

"Don't blame him!"

Frankie broke in. "All this romance is OK, but it doesn't solve where we'll have our sleepover for Hallowe'en."

"We must all be really, really nice, and get round our mums," said Lyndz, who reckoned being 'nice' was the answer to everything.

"Why don't we tell each mum that she's

the only one making a fuss?" said Fliss (whose mum usually *was* the only one making a fuss).

But Frankie came from a household of lawyers. "We could present our parents with a petition," she suggested.

"Won't work on my mum," Fliss moaned.

"Well, being ultra nice will only make mine suspicious," retorted Frankie.

"Why don't we try all our ideas?" suggested Rosie, and in the end that's what we agreed to.

A triple whammy.

The Sleepover Club was in danger and we had to pull out all the stops to save it. I don't mind telling you, I was worried. But that wasn't the only thing getting to me...

Merlin still hadn't been found.

Merlin my darling little pet had been missing for days. I was in a right state. That's why when I found The Evidence under my sister's bed, I nearly went through the bedsprings with excitement.

Here's how it happened.

I was under Molly's bed, looking for dirty socks, 'cos Frankie reckoned toe jam would make my 'Love Potion' extra potent! Anyway, there I was, wondering why Molly kept chewed-up paper and shredded tissues under her bed, when I noticed a brown, lumpy pile. (Not what you're thinking.) This was a secret stash of chocolate brazils piled up like rocks, one on top of the other. It was a mini-wall built so painstakingly, it looked like a fortification from a cartoon about knights.

Chewed-up paper? Shredded tissues? Chocolate nut walls?

No one but my clever Merlin could've done it and the tiny teeth marks in the chocolate were a big clue. But as if that wasn't enough, Merlin's sneaky little trail of rat droppings, all the way up to Molly's slipper, proved it.

Merlin, my clever little wall builder, you are alive!

I was dying to break the good news to my sister. But I decided to wait until that night when she was all nicely tucked up in bed.

"Molly?" I began.

"Go to sleep."

"Molly..."

"*What*!?"

"You know those chocolate brazils you accused me of stealing?"

"Yeah, and I know you took them. So don't try to get round Mum with your goody-goody housework tricks..."

"Actually I didn't steal them," I said airily. "Someone much smaller than me did."

"Shut up."

"Someone much smaller... with tiny pink paws and a long skinny tail..."

Molly's duvet froze.

"Yes. Did you know that someone with a long twitchy nose is hoarding your chocolate brazils?"

"H-hoarding them?" whispered a muffled voice from under the duvet. "Wh... where?"

"UNDER YOUR BED!" I hissed. Then I yawned extra loudly and snuggled down to sleep. "Goodnight, Molly."

My sister was grey the next morning. The thought that Merlin was loose in her bedroom was probably torment to a rat-hater like her. (Serves her right!) The silly thing was so anxious to catch Merlin that she didn't say a word when I built a trap for him with her precious chessboard.

Molly's chessboard made an ace ramp, leaned up against a bucket. I planted a trail of chocolate brazils all the way up the ramp so when Merlin reached the top, he'd keel over and drop into the bucket – PLOP! I made a nest of cotton wool for a soft landing and buried a bonus chocolate, just to reward my little pet.

But clever Merlin took the bait much quicker than even I had expected. 'Cos, ten minutes later, I was on the loo when there was an almighty CRASH! Then a scuffle and a bloodcurdling scream.

"Aaargh! KENNY! HELP!"

I shot off the loo so fast, there wasn't time to pull up my knickers. But Merlin was even faster! He zoomed about the bedroom like a jet-propelled rocket. Round and round he scampered, climbing up the curtains, skittering across the pelmet and haring along the picture rail at record speed. I chased and he raced and all the time Molly crouched in the corner of her bed, screaming her silly head off.

"Aaargh! Aaaargh! Aaaaaargh!"

It went on for ages. Then, suddenly Merlin disappeared behind the bedside table.

"Aargh!" shrieked Molly again, shrinking further into the corner of her bed.

"It's no good," I said, flopping down on my bed. "If you hadn't kicked the bucket over and screamed yourself silly, Merlin'd be safe and sound by now."

"C-couldn't h-help it."

"The only way is to leave him alone here. He'll come out when it's quiet."

"B-but that means I'll have to walk across the floor," said Molly, looking as if she had to walk the plank.

I shrugged. "Either that, or stay where you are until Merlin appears."

Molly pulled her duvet up to her chin.

"Oh… but Molly?"

"Wh-what?"

"If you do stay in bed all day, you'd better remember one thing…"

"What?"

"Rats are *very good climbers*."

* * *

It was irresistible. When I came back into the bedroom after breakfast, there was Molly, with her stomach bare, snoring like a rhino. (She had to catch up on her missed sleep from last night, poor thing.) Anyway, the chance to get a bit of fluff from her belly button was too good to miss. I'd got hair, nail clippings and toe jam – but so far, *no fluff*.

Stealthily as a witch's cat, I crept up... leaned over... and ever so, ever so gently *tweaked*...

"*Aaaargh*!" Molly leapt up screaming like a scalded cat. "Aaargh, aaargh!"

The earpiercing screams alerted Mum, who bounded up the stairs and burst into the bedroom. "What on earth's going on?"

"Rats!" Molly shrieked. "R-rats crawling all over me..."

Mum sighed. "It was probably just a dream, love."

"B-but they were all over me."

"Just a dream."

"It wasn't."

Dunno why, but seeing Molly all white and shaky made me want to put her out of her misery. "It wasn't rats. I was just..."

Molly turned on me, ungrateful as ever. "It was you! *You, you, you!*"

"Now stop it, Molly," said Mum.

"But *Mu-um*! Kenny — "

Mum held up her hand. "I've had enough of this. Kenny has been really trying lately. Cleaning up your mess... Helping out around the house..."

Molly glared at me.

"It's time you two called a truce..." Mum pleaded so hopefully that I acted nicer than even Lyndz might have expected.

"Don't worry Miss Rat-Hater," I muttered. "Merlin is safely in his cage again." No thanks to you! I thought crossly.

But Molly was not ready to give up the fight. "Where was the slimy, horrible thing?"

"In the bucket," I said. "My trap worked like a dream."

"Yeuch!" shivered Molly. Some people are never grateful.

"There!" said Mum, squeezing Molly's shoulders. "Now you can stop dreaming about rats, Molly. I think you ought to thank your sister." And as she said it, Mum flashed me one of her 'darling daughter' smiles.

No doubt about it, I was Mum's blue-eyed girl these days. Though I must admit it felt like I'd won through false pretences.

Still, false pretences or not, when Mum suggested a Hallowe'en sleepover in the famous McKenzie caravan, how could I refuse?

"*A sleepover in the caravan*!"

"I said 'no sleepovers in the house', but our caravan is parked in the driveway, so perhaps that doesn't count," explained Mum with a twinkle in her eye.

I almost knocked over my plate of Spaghetti Hoops in my rush to hug my mum. "Mum, you're a *star*!"

"It's only for Hallowe'en," warned Mum. "You're still banned from the house."

"I know!" I rushed to the phone to tell the gang how Lyndsey's 'being nice' idea had worked. "This is going to be the best Hallowe'en ever!" I cheered.

But Fliss was not so enthusiastic. "A sleepover in the McKenzie caravan!" she shivered. "It's probably full of spiders!"

"We can use them for Hallowe'en," Frankie teased.

"I'm not sleeping there!" insisted Fliss.

"Well we can't have our sleepover at your house," I retorted. "Not with the 'Teething Twins'."

Fliss had to admit this was true.

"Mine's out too," Frankie reminded us. "My mum and dad are going to a Hallowe'en party and they said our gang's too much for any babysitter."

"My mum's gone all weird about the Sleepover Club ever since she bumped into Jilly's mum," said Lyndz. "But Kenny? Isn't the caravan haunted?"

"*Don't!*" whispered Fliss.

"Not any more," I said. "We went camping in it last summer and had a great time."

"Well, I think it's perfect for our Hallowe'en spells," said Rosie, who still preferred not to have sleepovers at her house.

And that decided it.

Our Hallowe'en sleepover was going to be in the famous McKenzie caravan.

Personally, I couldn't wait.

CHAPTER NINE

"Frankie, can you pin on my wings?" I asked.

"Wait 'til I finish sticking on my witch's talons," came Frankie's muffled voice from behind her witch mask.

"I'll do it," offered Lyndz, ever helpful. Though she made the whole caravan shake as she clumped over in her riding boots.

"Woof, woof!"

"Pepsi, stop rocking the boat!" Pepsi was jumping about like a mad thing, and making the caravan rock even more.

"Woof, woof!"

Yes, you guessed it! We were in the

caravan dressing up in our Hallowe'en costumes.

Hallowe'en at last!

Everyone had got fantastic costumes. Fliss was a fairy in a pink (natch!) tutu from her ballet class. Her mum had curled her blonde hair into ringlets and she even had a sparkly tiara on top. She looked dead good. Rosie was a white witch (that means she was a good one) in one of her mum's nighties and Lyndz was a jockey in jodhpurs and riding hat. Frankie, as you know, was the famous wicked witch who had scared Molly before…

And me? Well, I was Cupid the love cherub who was going to shoot my lurrrrrrve arrow straight into the heart of Molly and Robin. Unfortunately the arrows were only rubber tipped! Though I say it myself, I looked fab with my curly clown's wig and tissue paper wings. I'd even got a plastic bow and arrow from an old Robin Hood costume. Mind you, Frankie reckoned if I really wanted to look like Cupid, I should go *starkers*!

Thank goodness dear old Rosie pointed out I'd freeze my bum off in this weather!

October in Leicester is not the best time for running round in skimpy costumes. That's why our mums made us promise to wear our school coats between houses when we went trick-or-treating. But nothing was gonna stop our gang having a wicked Hallowe'en.

Mind you, Frankie was not keen on doing trick-or-treat at all at first. She reckoned we were too old for all that baby stuff. But Lyndz, who couldn't miss out on the chance for sweets, won her over. She said it'd be cool if we only went to friends' and neighbours' houses.

"Does Robin Hughes count?" I asked, aiming an arrow at his imaginary heart.

"'Course," said Fliss, waving her sparkly wand about. "He's my neighbour, isn't he?"

Fliss was right. And luckily that made my plan to save the Sleepover Club easier.

Soon all our troubles would be over. Molly would give up swimming and go to Chess Club, Mum's ban would be over and Silly Jilly would never have to sleep over at our house again!

The Sleepover Club

We had our spell-making Hallowe'en Sleepover all planned out.

1. Dress up in caravan
2. Trick-or-treat
3. Get Robin Hughes' fingerprint
4. Cast spells
5. Eat Hallowe'en sweets
6. Tell ghost stories
7. Eat more sweets
8. Stay up
9. Eat loads more sweets!
10. Oh yes, and go to sleep some time

By 7.30pm, we'd nearly finished number two of our list. We'd visited our houses and our neighbours' houses and got a ton of goodies. Our bags were bursting!

Fliss's street was the last to go...

"Thanks, Mrs Proudlove!"

"Happy Hallowe'en!"

"Sssh, guys," Fliss's mum waved at us from the doorway. "Don't wake the twins."

"Sorry!" we mouthed, and crept back down the pathway, clutching our bags of goodies.

Outside the gate, we slipped our coats back on, swapped sweets and wondered whether to knock on the Grumpies' door. The Grumpies are Fliss's snooty neighbours, the Watson-Wades, and they don't get their nickname for nothing! They're so fussy about their posh house, our gang's always getting into trouble with them. The best time was when we threw toast, waffles and porridge into their garden and they landed in the Grumpies' prized pond! But that's another story…

"It's no good asking *them* for sweets," Fliss sighed, probably remembering the earwigging she got from her mum over the Grumpies. "Mrs Watson-Wade says sweets are nasty sticky things and she wouldn't have them in her house."

"So…" Frankie was sucking on a ginormous gobstopper, "we should play a trick on them!"

"Like what?"

"T.P. their house."

"What's that?" asked Rosie, unwrapping another treacle toffee.

"T.P. stands for toilet paper," said Frankie with a grin.

"And it means we wrap their house in toilet paper. The roof, the tree, everything," I added.

"Don't be daft, Kenny!" said Rosie with her mouth full. "How could we climb…?"

But she didn't have time to finish, because Frankie-the-witch was already creeping up the Grumpies' driveway.

NEENAH! NEENAH!

Suddenly alarm bells went off and lights floodlit the garden. Dogs barked and the whole place was lit up like a prison camp in one of those old war films. The door to the Grumpies' house was flung open and the Proudlove twins started bawling loud enough to wake the Hallowe'en dead!

"SCARPER!" hissed Frankie, so the five of us legged it down the driveway and up the street. And before Mr Watson-Wade had time to shout, "Pack of wild animals!" we had disappeared round the corner.

"That was close!" panted Frankie.

"I'm not going back there," Fliss said breathlessly.

Me neither. We had enough to do without getting arrested by the Grumpies for disturbing the peace. For a start, we needed to collect a fingerprint from Robin Hughes.

Holding on to my side, I panted, "Fliss, have you got the cupcakes for Robin?"

Fliss nodded and opened a tin of scrummy chocolate cupcakes. Yum, yum! Mrs Proudlove may be strict about keeping her kitchen clean, but she is an ace cook! Little did she know how her cooking was going to help save the Sleepover Club...

The Hughes' house didn't have any burglar alarms, but the nerd himself still looked surprised to see us.

"Hello, Robin," said Fliss, putting on her soppy 'fairy' voice.

Robin was too interested in Frankie's mask to notice Fliss's fairy outfit. "We don't have any sweets," he said, staring at the mask. "My mum doesn't believe in sugar."

"You can have some of ours..." Fliss opened the tin of cupcakes. "Your mum won't mind these, 'cos they're homemade."

"Thanks!" Robin licked his lips. Then he picked the biggest cupcake and took such a huge bite he got chocolate all over his big nose.

Frankie snorted behind her mask and Lyndz started to giggle. But it gave me a perfect chance. "Wait!" I grabbed the cake.

"*Hey*!" protested Robin.

"Er… sorry. That's the one the dog licked," I lied. I put the cupcake very carefully back in the tin. "Have another one instead."

Robin looked puzzled but he scoffed another cupcake anyway. (Some boys may be clever, but girls can still get one over them.)

"Molly sent her love to you," was my parting shot to the Chess Wiz. And underneath the globs of chocolate his face turned pink.

"What are you going to do with that cake Robin started?" asked Rosie as we turned the corner.

"Mix it in the Love Potion, of course."

"Why?" Rosie can be so dim sometimes.

"Because it has his thumb print on it, Lame Brain!"

"Ohhhh. Clever."

"You said it!" My plan was going so well that I almost danced down the street.

Lyndz started to giggle. "What about when Robin got chocolate all over his nose?"

"I think some even went up it."

"Eeeuw." Fliss made out she was being sick. "That cake's probably got his snot all over it!"

"Or a big bogey…"

"What a nerd."

We fell about the pavement, killing ourselves. "What a nerdy nerd nerd!"

That's when Rosie went haywire. She started waving her arms about, shouting, "*The Curse of the Nerd's Nose! The Curse of the Nerd's Nose!*" and chased us down the street.

The five of us raced, yelling like mad, all through the dark streets of Cuddington… and all the way back to the caravan.

The caravan looked magic in the candlelight. Mum had given us candle holders and shown me where it was safe to stand them, and we had draped fake spider webs everywhere. We'd stuck glow-in-the-dark pumpkins and ghosts all over the walls and Lyndz had tied a magic wreath to the caravan's door handle. She'd made it with straw from the stables and ivy from her back garden.

"It will bring us fairy luck," she said, and Fliss did a little bit of fairy ballet, just to be sure.

"Fliss, you're s'posed to say:

"Come in from the mist of silvery dew,
Come gather dance and play,
Pixies, elves and fairies too
Come to us today,"

Lyndz chanted.

"I did already. I said it on my own in my garden." Fliss was still nervous about doing spells.

Not me. I think Hallowe'en is coo-ell!

So does Frankie. She loved all the mystery and witchcraft and she wanted to do a Broomstick Incantation before we got started on our spells, to make the caravan more magical. So we sat in a magic circle on the floor and watched while she got herself into a witchy mood. Frankie's blue plastic kitchen broom didn't look much like a witch's broomstick, but as Rosie said, "a broom is a broom".

"Now for my incantation," Frankie muttered, dead creepy-like.

"Uh-oh."

"Sshh!" hissed Frankie as Lyndz started giggling.

"Sorry." Lyndz clapped her hand over her mouth so hard she got the hiccups. "Hic! Hic!"

Uh-oh. Once Lyndsey Collins gets the hiccups, that's it. We tried scaring her and making her hold her breath, but it was no good. In the end, Frankie said she we'd have to ignore her or we'd be here 'til next Hallowe'en.

So apart from the occasional 'hic', everything went quiet. In the eerie candlelight Frankie tied a green ribbon on her broom handle. Then she tied a yellow one next to it. Dead tricky with witch's talons glued to your fingernails, so it took an extra long time.

"Pretty!" said Fairy Fliss when it was done. And she tapped the broom with her sparkly wand.

"The yellow ribbon's s'posed to be gold," Frankie explained, "but I couldn't find any. Ooops! I forgot, I'm supposed to say something while I'm tying the ribbons!" So Frankie had to untie the ribbons and start all over again. This time she chanted:

> *"This caravan is filled with magic,*
> *And this broom is my lucky charm."*

It made you shiver. Especially when Frankie closed her eyes and walked round our magic circle with the broom stuck out in front of her.

"What are you doing now?" Rosie wanted to know.

"Sweeping away unwanted energy... Clearing away for the new..." Frankie whispered in a strange voice.

"*Ouch!*"

"Sorry," said Frankie who'd stepped on Lyndsey's hand.

"Hic!"

Frankie sighed and closed her eyes to concentrate. Then she turned round and round on the spot, sweeping around herself in one big circle, and chanting:

> *"Here I sweep,*
> *Round and round,*

Drawing a magic circle
On the ground."

We were all getting totally spooked when Frankie snapped open her eyes and announced in her normal voice, "That's it."

We all jumped.

"It's dead magical in here now!"

"Coo-ell!"

It did feel magic. Our gang is so good at Pretend you end up believing it.

Next it was Lyndsey's turn for her Merrylegs spell. She had all the stuff for it, but the trouble is, Lyndz can't be serious about anything. When she started pawing in the sprinkled sand, she hiccuped so much she got the giggles big time. So we all made horsey noises to help her along.

"Neeeeeigh…"

Dunno if spells work when you're mucking about, but Lyndz was ever hopeful. "Now all I have to do is wait for my horse."

"How long?" Rosie looked round the caravan as if expecting the horse to gallop in any minute.

"Dunno," said Lyndz.

Rosie had already done her spell, so she didn't need to do any more. She'd had to thread shells and bells on to two long bits of thread and hang one each outside her own house and her dad's. "It's s'posed to help bring peace and harmony in divorced homes," she explained.

Nobody said anything. We knew how much this meant to Rosie and we hoped, for her sake, it worked.

Next it was Frankie's turn to do Pepsi's Puppy Spell. Pepsi was dead good when Frankie tied bits of pink and blue wool to her tail, and she wagged it like mad when it was finished. But when it came to turning three times in the middle of the circle, the daft dog was hopeless. She thought it was a game and kept trying to jump on to Frankie's lap.

"Stay, Pepsi! Stay!"

Pepsi sat down obediently and wagged her decorated tail.

"Now turn around. Turn around, Pepsi."

Pepsi leapt up and lunged at Frankie, bowling her over and licking her witch's mask.

"Woof, woof!"

"Pepsi, you're never going to have puppies at this rate," Frankie-the-witch laughed.

And the Sleepover gang had to agree.

CHAPTER TEN

At last. Time for my Love Spell.

A thrill went right through me.

While the rest of the gang chanted *"Robin, Molly, Robin, Molly,"* I mixed my powerful Love Potion in a plastic beaker:

1. One toenail (Molly's)
2. Scrap of belly button fluff
3. Crumb of toe jam
4. One long hair
5. One half-eaten cupcake with thumbprint
6. Teaspoon of rainwater to moisten

I did a bit of swaying with my eyes closed, to make it more real, and muttered witchy - type things. I don't know how long I was supposed to do it, but when the potion felt all gloppy and mixed, I set it carefully in the middle of the circle.

Rosie inspected it. "This'd be a wicked mixture for a Sleepover dare." (Rosie was probably remembering the time she had to eat 'Nappy's Brains' to get into the Sleepover Club.)

"Yuck!"

"*Sssh!*" I scratched the initials 'R' and 'M' either end of the red candle I'd got in Harmony Heaven. Then I broke the candle in half and rubbed the two bits of it together, just for good luck.

"Ahhh, it's like they're kissing..." sighed Fliss.

"We have to do the next part outside," I said.

"Why?"

"My mum said we weren't to play with candles in the caravan."

There was a bit of grumbling about the cold, but in the end, we all put on our school coats and trooped out into the dark.

"Get into a circle again," I commanded.

They all huddled together, looking very unmagical.

"It's cold!" Fliss complained.

Honestly. "Are we doing this or not?" I huffed.

So the gang formed a disgruntled circle.

I lit the two pieces of candle. Then, slowly, slowly I began dripping wax from each burning piece into the Love Potion. The melted wax sizzled and turned into red blobs the second it hit the potion.

"Cool! Looks like drops of blood."

"Eeuch!"

Ignoring them, I went on dripping. Drip, drip, stir and chant. Drip, drip, stir and chant:

> *"Come Robin, come to Molly.*
> *You know why, but can't deny*
> *Your need to come to Molly.*

> *"Come Molly, come to Robin.*
> *You know why, but can't deny*
> *Your need to come to Robin."*

Everything felt suddenly real, especially when the moon went behind a cloud. It was very cold and very very dark.

Fliss shivered. "Feels like we're being watched. Let's go back inside."

Was it the moon, or the wind whispering in the bushes? But I felt it too and so did the others. Without another word, we stumbled back up the caravan steps. Fast.

Inside the caravan, I set the potion in the middle of the circle. Then I chanted the extra bit I'd made up, just to save our Sleepover Club:

> *"Molly and Robin, Robin and Molly,*
> *Meet at Chess Club on Saturdays.*
> *Leave our Sleepover Club alone,*
> *And stop your sneaky ways!"*

Suddenly there was a low ghostly moan, and the caravan began to shake.

"Wh-what's that?" Fliss quavered.

Softly at first, the caravan shook, then more and more, until the whole thing was swaying like a boat out at sea. Pepsi whimpered, Fliss screamed and Lyndz's hiccups disappeared.

The moaning went on... Then along the sides of the caravan was a scrabbling sound, scrabble, scrabble, scrabble, as if hundreds and thousands of long bony fingers were clawing to get in.

"Wh-what is it?"

We were too terrified to do anything but cling together for dear life, trembling like mad. And the moaning was getting louder.

After the longest two minutes in our whole lives, Lyndz had a brainwave. "F-Fliss, call my brother!" she whispered.

"H-how?"

"On your mobile!"

Fliss usually had her mobile with her the whole time. But her fairy costume had nowhere to keep her mobile, so we were out of luck.

"I want my mum!" cried Fliss.

"Frankie, you and Kenny run to the house!" said Rosie.

"No way," Frankie trembled.

"Send Pepsi with a note, then."

But Pepsi was cowering against Frankie's leg. She was going nowhere.

We couldn't go out and we couldn't stay there. What could we do?

Hide? Faint? Die of fright? Probably. We'd be found years later, five frozen girls and a spaniel with bows on her tail.

There was only one thing left to do.

Together we took deep breaths and opened our mouths. In one long shriek we screamed louder and longer than we've ever screamed before. We screamed and screamed and screamed, until it felt like we'd never ever stop.

"*Aaaaaaaaaaaaargh!*"

And that's when slowly, very slowly, the door to the caravan creaked open.

CHAPTER ELEVEN

"DAD!"

Mega-relieved, I flung myself at my dad, and held on to him tight.

But Dad wasn't feeling so loving. "*What in heaven's name is going on here!*" he yelled.

Everyone tried to answer, but their voices were drowned by my dad's yelling. Dad's explosions don't come often, but when they do – watch out! He shouted that he could hear our screaming all the way from the back bedroom. And just in case he couldn't, the next-door neighbours had phoned to tell him all about it. "You've probably woken half the neighbourhood!" Dad hollered in a voice loud enough to wake the other half.

"Sorry..."

"I don't know what you think you're playing at..."

"Just having a bit of Hallowe'en fun, Dad..."

"Hallowe'en or not, you *blah, blah, blah...*"

Dad went on and on.

I thought he'd never stop.

Only good thing was, Molly and Jilly got it in the neck even more than the Sleepover Club. Dad reckoned their silly behaviour could've have caused a major accident, with all the candles and 'nonsense'. Candle holders or no candle holders, fire was dangerous stuff and he would speak to Mum about it.

Yes, in case you hadn't guessed, it was not witches or ghouls that had given us the fright of our lives. It was my dear sister and her silly friend. And if Molly and Jilly thought they'd *win* by scaring us with ghostly tricks like shaking the caravan, they were wrong. Dad told them so in no uncertain terms.

Finally Dad stomped off to get on the phone to the other parents.

Whew!

But in less than half an hour the grown-ups had come to pick up their 'naughty' daughters, and everyone, including Jilly, was taken home.

Ooops.

The only one left was Frankie. Her mum and dad were out, so Dad had to let her to stay. He wasn't best pleased about that, either. 'Course, it wasn't the sleepover we'd planned, but at least, me and my best friend were together, while Molly the Monster had to share with Emma. One nil to the Sleepover Club!

Before Dad could go on any more, me and Frankie did our famous getting-ready-for-bed race (one minute two seconds!) and leapt into bed. When Dad came up to check on us we were already hiding under our duvets.

"Frankie, I'll speak to your parents tomorrow," Dad said as he snapped out the bedroom light, leaving us in total darkness.

I waited 'til he'd gone downstairs. "What do you think your mum and dad'll do?" I whispered to Frankie.

"Boil me in oil… Tear me from limb to limb…"

"No, really."

"Dunno. Pass me the sweets."

We needed some comfort after Dad's ear-wigging. So we had our own Sleepover mini-feast and told each other jokes. Here are a couple, just to cheer you up:

Question: What do you get when you mix a cross witch with ice cubes?
Answer: A cold spell.

Question: How do witches drink tea?
Answer: With a cup and sorcerer.

And Frankie's favourite:

Sign at a Witches' Demo:
"We demand Sweeping Reforms!"

Did they make you laugh? They did us. (You know how you get the giggles after you've been in trouble? Well, we did. Big Time.) We couldn't stop. I think we fell asleep laughing, just when the bedroom was beginning to get light again…

Thank goodness for Frankie.

*   *   *

My best friend didn't get boiled in oil, or torn limb from limb, but she got grounded. The whole gang did. No more visits, no more sleepovers, no more fun until next year. Dad said he'll see if we're grown up enough for sleepovers by then. (Huh!) Still, as Frankie pointed out, we've had that threat before. And grown-ups have got very short memories, sometimes. Have you noticed that? I think they've even forgotten it's nearly Christmas, so next year's not that long to wait.

Anyway, don't get worried. The grown-ups can't stop the Sleepover gang from having fun. 'Fun' is our middle name. And they can't stop us having a fab, fab Christmas. Frankie says we have the right to sue them if they try that.

At school, things are really coo-ell too. Mrs Weaver is letting us plan a sooper-dooper Christmas party, so our class is dead excited. We're decorating the classroom and bringing food and CDs and playing games. It's gonna be ace. Then there's the Nativity play and the Carol Service...

It was at the school Carol Service that the grown-ups started to soften. Probably the sight of their little darlings dressed as angels did it. All the mums had got those soppy smiles grown-ups always get at the school Nativity play and Carol Service. So I thought I'd make the most of it, by handing round the mince pies in my angel costume.

"Mince pie, Mrs Proudlove?" I said sweetly.

"Thank you, Laura," smiled Fliss's mum. "That was beautiful singing, just now."

"Thank you."

"Yes. A much better sound than screaming," said Mum with a twinkle in her eye.

"*Mu-um*!" I groaned. "That was ages and ages ago. We haven't had a single sleepover since Hallowe'en."

The mums gave each other one of those looks that said, 'Good thing too!'.

"It's not fair!" Frankie in her angel's wings looked as if she was about to take off. "We've got rights!"

Her mum looked at her fondly. Then she spoke up. "The Sleepover Club means a lot to them. Perhaps they've learnt their lesson."

"We have," chimed in Fliss, her angel costume billowing round her. "We'll never do spells again."

"Promise," added Rosie.

"Pleeeease can we have a Christmas sleepover?" begged Lyndz, putting her hands together like she was praying. Which looked dead good with her halo and stuff. "Please, please, please?"

The mums looked at one another again. Then my mum said the magic words:

"*We'll see.*"

And you know what that means in Adult Speak, don't you?

YAY! One nil to the Sleepover Club!

Mind you, Fliss was telling the truth when she said we wouldn't do any more spells. We were being right little goody goodies these days. But that didn't stop the spells we did on Hallowe'en from working their magic. And, messing about or not, some of them did work in a funny kind of way.

For a start, Rosie reckons things at home are more peaceful. Her brother Adam (the one with cerebral palsy) has a spiffy new wheelchair, and he's practising a brilliant new wheelie routine in it for Christmas. And Rosie's mum's boyfriend has promised to paint their hall in the new year, so the place won't look so much of a bomb site. Of course, Rosie's dad isn't back with her mum, but, as I reminded her, spells are only spells. Not miracles.

Lyndz hasn't got her horse yet but Frankie's giving her one from her miniature collection for Christmas, so in a way Lyndz will get her wish. (And don't tell Frankie, but I bought her a cute little china puppy for Christmas. It cost a whole week's pocket money, but I reckon my best friend is worth it.)

Oh, you want to know about Fliss, too? Well, she hasn't seen fairies at the bottom of her garden yet, but (secretly) I think she's still looking. Fliss got it the worst of all of us, really. Her mum took the spell-making stuff deadly seriously and it didn't matter how much Fliss explained it was 'just fun', Mrs Proudlove was furious. She said witchcraft was 'dangerous mischief' and she docked Fliss's pocket money. Mind you, Fliss gets so much pocket money, that only makes her in the same boat as all of us now.

I s'pose the spell stuff did get a teeny weeny bit out of hand… But like I told you before, the Sleepover gang is mega good at Pretend. So good that, believe it or not, my Love Potion did work some kind of magic.

It happened like this…

On the day of Molly's swimming gala, Mum made me go with her to cheer Molly on. "It's time you buried the hatchet and gave you sister some support," she said firmly.

True enough, my sneaky sister could do with some help. Molly has been what my mum calls 'spreading herself thin' lately. She's been going to Chess Club one week and swimming the next, so now her swimming speed's rubbish. Still, with her own school pool she doesn't have to rely on summer openings at the public baths like we do at our school. So Molly can practise in the new year to get back up to her 'Olympic Standard' (ha, ha).

At the pool, I did my best to cheer her on, for Mum's sake. I shouted and waved and whistled, like a real fan. I've had plenty of practice at that when I go to Leicester City football matches. So I got into the act. But the funny thing was, as I got into shouting and clapping like mad, *I really began to feel it*.

Suddenly I wanted Molly to swim well. I wanted her to beat the others and I wanted her to win like mad.

"Come on, Molly!" I shouted. "WIN! WIN! WIN!"

She didn't win of course. But when she came fifth... guess who was waiting on the sidelines to comfort her?

Robin Hughes!

Yes, the Chess Wiz himself actually praised Molly's effort, and what's more, *Molly seemed to like it*. (Heh, heh, maybe I am a witch after all...)

So, the Sleepover Club actually got a boy interested in Molly the Monster. Will wonders never cease? It only goes to prove, what I've said before... The Sleepover Club can do anything!

Wonder what we'll do next?
Think I'll just take a look in my crystal ball...

Mega Sleepover Club ⑥

In Sleepover Girls go Snowboarding, the gang tries to stay cool on the slopes – with disastrous results!

In Merry Christmas Sleepover Club, Cinderella is the school panto – but who will get the leading role?

And in Happy New Year Sleepover Club, Frankie's baby sister is born in the middle of the biggest New Year's Eve party ever!

Three wonderful wintery
Sleepover Club stories in one!

www.harpercollins.co.uk
Visit the book lover's website

Mega Sleepover Club 7

Mega news! The crazy Spanish students the Sleepover Club met on holiday are coming to stay in *Sleepover Girls and Friends* – but there's trouble ahead with the M&Ms. It's wedding bells for Fliss's mum in *The Sleepover Club Bridesmaids*, and the gang have a huge role to play. Will the arrival of ghastly Amber ruin their plans? And in *Sleepover Girls on the Ball*, sneaking into the posh Green Lawns Tennis Club seems like a good idea, but will fun in the sun turn into major disaster...?

Three sizzling summery Sleepover Club stories in one!

Collins

www.harpercollins.co.uk
Visit the book lover's website

Order Form

To order direct from the publishers, just make a list of the titles you want and fill in the form below:

Name ....

Address ....

....

....

Send to: Dept 6, HarperCollins Publishers Ltd, Westerhill Road, Bishopbriggs, Glasgow G64 2QT.

Please enclose a cheque or postal order to the value of the cover price, plus:

UK & BFPO: Add £1.00 for the first book, and 25p per copy for each additional book ordered.

Overseas and Eire: Add £2.95 service charge. Books will be sent by surface mail but quotes for airmail despatch will be given on request.

A 24-hour telephone ordering service is available to holders of Visa, MasterCard, Amex or Switch cards on 0141- 772 2281.

An imprint of HarperCollins*Publishers*